In memory of my mother Barbara Ann McCullars Kendall who I took after in the writing department.

In memory of my brothers Kevin, Bill, and Kenneth Kendall.

Thanks and love to my closest friend Jason Burkhardt who has helped me with some of the content.

My love to my son Dustin Thomas who has been there when I needed someone to talk to.

My love to my sister Ro Hennen, and my father Roy Kendall who has found time to be there for me through some tough times.

My love to my brother Paul Kendall and his wife Charlotte Kendall, two incredibly special people in my life.

My love to my youngest sister Kathy McCabe who is the apple of my eye and her husband Mike McCabe.

My love to my nephew Robert Provan who we are very blessed to have in our lives.

My prayers and love to a very special lady, Vanessa Schlesinger, and her family.

To Find The Rose

This novel is a work of fiction. Names, characters, places, and incidents either are the products of the author's imagination or are used fictitiously. Any resemblance to actual events, locales, or persons, living or dead, is entirely coincidental.

Cover Design: SelfPubBookCovers.com/DillsDesigns

Chapter 1

Susan Mullican examined her reflection in the store window. She had to look her best for the first day on the job; more like the first day on a new mission. One she prayed would prove to be successful. Too many failed ones behind her.

Out of the three other stores she worked at in the past year, the first one was more promising. Until she got kicked out. The last two, unfortunately, were dead ends.

Why the person at the first one called her a spy was beyond her. If anyone were one, it would be *him.*

That was a year ago, and now she had to go forward believing she would find what she had been promised.

The olive blouse she chose to go with the white skirt and white pumps helped hide the color in her face caused by the nervousness in her stomach.

She hoped this was the last store she would encounter. Susan always thought lowly of bargain stores and working at them only confirmed that. She would tell of her dreadful experiences to her little sister, Rose.

Rose. That now familiar tugging overtook Susan's heart. She was the reason for Susan being at the bargain store in the first place.

No time for that thought now. Summoning up the Mullican backbone, she straightened up. The cool autumn breeze teased her curly auburn hair while taking in one last glance at her image. She was ready to meet her new boss, Barbara Davis.

Inside the store she had a hard time locating Barbara. There were plenty of black-haired ladies, but most of them were shorter than she remembered Ms. Davis from her job interview the other day.

She scanned the large room. The five-foot tall glass shelves holding various knickknacks allowed her to spot her new manager waiting on a man at the counter.

Susan's gaze met Barbara's brown eyes. Barbara waved at her, then motioned a blonde-haired lady to step in her place.

Barbara gave Susan a warm greeting.

"I'm so glad you made it. As you can see this may be a small five and dime store, but we get a lot of customers. I will give you the rundown while we wait for our accountant to arrive to do your paperwork.

"Our employees mainly consist of our stocker Joey, the other cashiers Linda and Melissa, the owners Jim and Kathy Boyd, I, and of course our accountant Craig Summers."

Susan knew an accountant at the first store she worked at by the name of Craig, but his last name was Bryers. That had been a hundred miles away, and he was one man she wanted desperately to forget about.

How could she? Her dreams kept him alive almost every tiresome night for a year. They started out with the pleasant, cordial side of him. Then he would flip and be unkind, but soft-spoken, telling her he did not want to be cruel to her, but he had to. That was a dream because the real Craig meant to be callous.

"Speaking of whom, here he is." A pleased voice drifted from Barbara. "Susan, I want you to meet Craig Summers. Craig, this is Susan Mullican. You'll recall she's starting work today."

Susan turned to face a man she knew all too well. Those deep golden eyes that once mystified and held her. His rustic appearances accented by the fragrance of Stetson cologne he wore. The soft, dark brown hair she used to run her hands through. And he still sported the Clark Gable mustache with the irresistible lips to match.

He was, in fact, Craig Bryers. By the expression on his face, he was just as surprised to see her.

"Hello, Ms. Mullican." The corner of his mouth quirked up at her as he reached out a hand and seized hers. "I hope you don't mind if we go to my office where it's quieter and do your paperwork."

The sound of her blood pulsing through her head pounded with each step she took as she kept in stride with him. The last encounter they had he threatened her life if she came around him again. She was not sure if he would carry out that threat.

She wanted to race out of there, but she had to go through with the orientation. To locate her sister her connection told her she would acquire what she needed there.

The office offered no windows... only a bookcase with notebooks, two chairs and a desk holding a computer and scattered papers.

She felt boxed in, like the room itself. Her breathing became shallow as Craig closed the door and turned to face her. He looked intently into her eyes.

"I thought it was understood we wouldn't see each other again." His tone, so sharp it cut through the silence in the room, put Susan more on edge.

"I had no idea you worked here. How could I? You changed your last name. Unless Summers really is your last name."

Her throat carried a lump she desperately tried to get rid of. He brought out a fear in her. Not only of uncertainty of what would happen to her now, but also of her remembering his touches, his kisses, and the longing they once shared.

The desire was one that her integrity would not let her have. Not now.

"Well, Miss Mullican, I guess there is no other alternative but to," he paused for a moment. His eyes winced in pain, then he reached up and rubbed the back of his neck. The tension between them got the better of him, although it could easily be resolved.

"But to let me go?" She did not want to leave. She wanted to continue her search.

He lowered his hand and glared at her. "No, I can't do that. You know too much about me, and I can't trust you."

"You can trust me. I promise our meeting again is a fluke and I had no intentions of running into you."

His eyes darted from side to side of her face, then his jaw relaxed some.

His hand shot out and he hooked his index finger under her chin. She flinched as he gently lifted her head until their eyes met.

He searched her eyes. Her mind tried feverishly to stay alert to his actions and words, but the scent of Stetson drifted up her nostrils playing tricks with her senses.

"You need to give me a better reason to believe you than our meeting again being a fluke."

Ever since she was a child, Susan had a hard time coming up with answers readily. What could she tell him? Definitely not the purpose of her being there.

"Okay, try this one. I'm not pursuing you because I treasure my life more than to put it in harm's way." The bitterness in her words hit home, and some softening surfaced in his eyes. She hoped he was remorseful for threatening her life at the other store.

"You do realize as long as you are working here you cannot tell any-one about me." He pressed his lips together.

"I-I won't. I promise."

"I believe you." He withdrew his finger from under her chin and moved to his desk.

"Now, Ms. Mullican, we need to do the paperwork before Ms. Davis wonders what is going on." He gave her a devilish grin before handing her some forms to fill out.

Instead of being focused on her writing, her thoughts were on their last encounter when he vowed to kill her if they met again. She believed the confrontation then was more an element of surprise than of wanting to actually harm her. He was hiding something and trying to keep her away.

What worried her more was the attraction she had to a man who would intimidate her for any reason. The feelings for him ran deeper than phys-ical. She could not put her finger on it, but she would keep her guard up, and not only against him.

She handed him her paperwork. "Okay, Mr. Bryers."

Reaching out he grasped her hand. "Summers." His voice was as firm as his grip. "If you plan on working here, remember my last name is Summers." It was a warning.

"Point well taken. I apologize and promise it won't happen again." She controlled her tone while managing a ragged smile. He released her hand then returned her smile with a broad one, mocking her.

"I'll be keeping my eyes on you. No screw ups, understand?"

"Yes, sir."

The smirk on his face disappeared. "I mean what I say."

She gave him an understanding nod as she left his office.

* * *

"Darn it!" Craig spat out between clenched teeth as he flung her paperwork on his already cluttered desk.

Why did she come here and take a chance of messing up what he worked hard on for so many years? To include the emotions he put behind him when he ordered her out of the first store. The feelings he could not keep as long as he was on this assignment.

Her coolness was one he had not seen in a woman for a long time. Her thin lips begun to quiver, but she kept it under control. The desire to taste them again was compelling, but he could not risk blowing his cover, or worse.

He should have stayed centered on the case at the first store instead of entertaining thoughts of the two of them. She was up to something then when he caught her in his office. Especially after her snooping around in his ledgers.

The day after that encounter he uncovered a note she had written to him. A cover-up he was sure of. He carried it as a reminder for him not to fall into the same trap.

She presented more trouble than he needed, which was his reason for not wanting to hire her. Only purpose for her being there hinged on his contact informing him she would be a key to unlock a door he found last year.

He would have to be careful. If she were a Cartel spy like his connection, it would be dangerous for her to have knowledge of what was going on. It was a chance he was willing to take to find some answers quick.

*　*　*

Susan wandered around the store while waiting for Barbara to assign her tasks.

"Sorry about that." She turned as Barbara walked up on her. "Had a few things to line up. I think this morning I am going to have you dusting the shelves. This will help you familiarize yourself more with the items in the store that we sell."

Susan followed her to one of the registrars where she retrieved a duster and handed it to Susan.

Barbara motioned her hand toward the front door.

"It is best to start by the doorway and make your way around the main floor."

Susan took off in the direction indicated and began her task.

She found herself thinking back to her sister's room while dusting a ceramic unicorn. Rose loved unicorns. Everything in her room, from the wallpaper to the nightlight she had to have at the age of eighteen, was done in them.

Susan could not forget the last confrontation they had in that room. All about Rose's employment at a bargain store. Susan told her she was wasting her time with such menial work, but Rose kept insisting Susan was wrong.

* * *

"Wrong! What do you mean I'm wrong, Rose? Tell me. What good could come out of working at a place like that?"

"Even though the store may not be a physical healing as you perceive," Rose threw at her big sister with hostility, "it soothes the soul," she finished with a sneer.

Susan gave a half laugh, half hack. "Soothes the soul! How, I'd like to know?" She stood in front of her little sister, her hands on her hips, daring her to come up with something that would justify her claim.

Rose's short blonde hair bounced as she almost skipped over to her unicorn lamp and rubbed its head as if it would give her luck.

"Well, look at this lamp. It may look like some dumb unicorn with a light stuck out of its head to you, but I found it at the store, and it soothes my soul. I think of all the people out in the world who find treasures at these shops and are so happy that it makes me happy. All the way down to my soul." Rose looked up and gave a sheepish grin as her blue eyes sparkled.

"You're just wasting your time at that place. Grow up and get a real job." On her way out of the room Susan threw up her hands muttering Rose was just a kid.

* * *

That had been over a year ago, and the last day she had seen Rose. Rose disappeared. Part of Susan wondered if she ran away from her.

"Where are you Rose?" Urgency held in her voice as the tears streamed down Susan's cheeks.

She quickly wiped the moisture from her face as the sound of footsteps coming towards her caught her attention.

"There you are Susan." Barbara approached with a bleached blonde lazily walking behind her. A hint of black in her roots showed the blonde's original hair color.

Susan's philosophy about women who bleached their hair was they were insecure about themselves, except one. Nurse Betty Trublood, who had been her co-worker at the hospital. Betty was a bright and dependable person who would be there when someone needed something, and usually already had it in her hands.

Susan kept in touch with Betty since the first day she started searching for Rose, even though John Lancett, the family friend, advised her not to keep in contact with anyone.

The requirement of putting her life as a nurse on hold while going in pursuit of her sister remained hard on her. The hardest part was running into the dead-end leads. She had hoped this lead did not end up the same way.

Barbara introduced the blonde as Linda, one of the cashiers at the store. Linda held out a limp hand with the expression of 'have to do this for the boss' as a weak smile toyed on her lips.

"Yeah. Hi."

Susan waited for her to say something else, but in vain. Could this be the woman's vocabulary? How did she manage to obtain a job here? Did Barbara feel sorry for her? Yet here she was working at a place she herself condemned to Rose.

"Hi Linda. It's nice to meet you." Susan took hold of the other woman's hand and gave it a warm handshake. The desire to work at the bargain store was nil, nevertheless, she would invest herself in this position.

The white blouse Linda wore presented a low-cut V-neck. A gold, cone-shaped shell dangled from a gold chain nestled in her cleavage.

"I like your necklace. I don't think I've seen one like that before."

Linda's hazel eyes lit up as she grasped the shell and moved it closer to Susan's view.

"That's what Craig said when he found it at an auction. He said it would go great with my collection I have at home."

Linda's words took her by surprise. Were Linda and Craig seeing each other?

"Well ladies, I hate to break this up," Barbara began, "but we do have a store to run."

When the two departed, Susan caught sight of Craig in the background gazing in their direction before taking off for his office. Had he been watching them? Watching her? Or maybe Linda.

Linda was attractive enough for Craig to date, but her personality lacked in an area Susan was sure would turn him away. Maybe she had not shown him that lackadaisical side.

She did not know where his attraction to Linda was, but she did not want anything to do with him again. She was only there for one purpose. To find her sister Rose.

Chapter 2

Susan left the store at her appointed time, mentally more wrecked than when she first entered. Seeing Craig again rattled her nerves, as well as her emotions. Feelings she would need to shake off in order to stay focused on finding Rose.

The top of the sun peaked above the apartment complex as she maneuvered and settled into her assigned parking spot. Taking her things from the car, she headed toward the apartment she rented after John Lancett told her Mike Holmes had a lead to this bargain store.

After a year of hearing about the undercover cop's leads, and not getting anywhere, she wanted proof this move would bring her closer to Rose. Mike had presented a sheet of paper with Rose's social security number indicating her last employment was The Five and Dime Store.

The downside to the news was she had not appeared for work in weeks, and they were unsure of what happened to her.

It was up to Susan to find out about her little sister working there, but in a discreet way. They did not want to take a chance of something happening to her as well.

That had been the first real evidence on Rose, renewing her faith in finding her. She was up to the challenge.

Susan was at her front door when her new friend, Mrs. Robertson, and her poodle, Lady, strolled up to her.

"Hi, Susan." The older woman always beamed. This time she carried something in her chubby hands.

"I knew you probably wouldn't cook today, with starting your new job and everything, so I hope you don't mind I baked this casserole for you. You look like you could use it." She glanced down at Susan's waistline.

Susan managed to stay fit through the years, but this past year with the search and worrying about her sister kept her appetite suppressed.

"That is sweet of you. Thank you. I am pretty tired, so if you will excuse me, I'll try it later and tell you how it is." Susan gave her a smile and patted Lady on the head. The pup returned the pat by licking her hand.

"Lady really likes you. Not many people can pet her. Usually she nips their hand." Mrs. Robertson's puffy cheeks bounced as she chuckled. Susan bid her friend goodnight, then turned and unlocked her door.

Apartments were not her preference, but she had to play the part of a woman in need of a job. At least that is what John told her when she first started this escapade. He said she would appear too conspicuous if she rented a luxury suite.

The small place resembled somewhat of a homelike environment. Everything she brought with her was unpacked in a couple of days. It looked organized. Something she could live in for a while.

She set the casserole Mrs. Robertson gave her on a little round table with four chairs. Quite a difference from a long elegant one she used to eat at with her sister.

The unexpected ring of the phone caused her heart to flutter. The familiar voice on the other end was Craig.

"What do you want?"

Hostility laced her tone. She did not trust his intentions.

"I called to let you know tomorrow is our auction day, and Ms. Davis will want you to come with us. She always does with new employees, so they will be involved with the company. It would be a good idea if you went."

"Tomorrow is Saturday. Those places are opened over the weekend?"

"Yes."

"Who is going if I may ask?" Susan toned down her voice, but this request caught her off guard.

"Ms. Davis and myself."

That was what she was afraid of. "No, I can't go with you."

"Why not?"

"Because" she started, searching in her mind for something quick to say. She could not tell him that her feelings for him caused her to be uneasy. Just hearing his voice brought back the old affections she had for him.

"It's hard for me to sit still in one of those places." That was a good reason she thought, until she heard him snickering. "Well it is," she insisted.

"Ms. Davis is not going to buy that, and neither will I. We'll see you tomorrow, Miss Mullican." In a somewhat amusing note, he added for her to enjoy the evening and hung up before she protested anymore.

She tossed the phone on the table. Throwing herself on the couch, she buried herself in the soft fluffy cushions.

Enjoy the evening he said. How could she? Up until that day she was handling her emotions sufficiently while trying to find her sister.

What was Craig doing at this store anyway? Did the first place discover the same dishonest thing about him that she did?

Why did she find those books? It was by accident. She was looking for--what was it? Oh yeah, the note about her feelings for him she slipped into his stack of folders while talking to him in his office. Later on she decided to retrieve the paper before he found it and wondered if he ever came across it and read it.

What would that matter now? That was a year ago, and things have changed since then. She had to figure a way out of going to that auction with Barbara and Craig. Especially with Craig.

He is calling again, she thought as the phone rang. Annoyed, she marched to it.

"Now what do you want?"

"Is this Susan Mullican?" The female voice asked with uncertainty.

Susan realized who it was, and felt her cheeks getting hot.

"Yes. I'm sorry. I thought you were someone else." The caller was Betty Trublood, her best friend and former co-worker from the hospital back home.

"Evidently. And apparently someone you didn't want to talk to." Betty tried to prod her into telling what was going on. She was in luck because she was the only person Susan would tell.

"Do you remember the accountant Craig Bryers at the first store I worked at?"

"How could I forget? He was all you talked about there for a while. I thought you two were headed for wedding bells, until you told me what you discovered about him."

"He's at this one, but this time he changed his last name to Summers."

Betty let out a gasp. "Oh my gosh, girl. Has he threatened you anymore?"

"No, just said he was keeping his eyes on me."

"Maybe you should tell John about him?"

"No. I hadn't told him about Craig, other than him working at the other store. Anyway, he told me he would be hard to reach, and he would be in touch with me as soon as possible."

"Do you want me to go to your parents' company and tell him to call you?"

"No, Betty. I'm not supposed to be keeping in contact with anyone."

"I don't like you being out there by yourself, hon. I've got a few days' vacation and will hop on a plane and be there in a flash."

Despite the seriousness of the situation, she chuckled to herself at Betty's East Texas drawl. Susan was born and raised in East Texas, but never acquired the accent.

"I appreciate it, but it is dangerous enough for me by myself. I can't get you involved in this uncertainty, not knowing what's going on."

"Uncertainty? I thought John said this was a for sure thing. Oh, hon, you need to get your tail back home."

"I can't. I have to find Rose. I have no knowledge of where she is, and what has happened to her. That's hard on me." Susan pleaded her case.

"I know she's your last living kin, but I am just so afraid for you."

Susan remained silent on her end of the phone. She did not know what to say to help ease the other woman's mind when she could not ease her own.

Betty withdrew a heavy breath. "You keep in touch with me, hon, you hear. Always remember I'll be here anytime you need me. Please be careful."

"I will, and thanks for calling. Bye."

It was hard for Susan to hang up. It was like closing the door to the only sane world known to her.

* * *

The shower helped wash away the restless night. As adamant as Craig was the night before about her going to the auction, she decided on wearing something casual. Lord knew she was not up to it, but she would rather be prepared in case she could not get out of it.

Once out the door, she ran into Mrs. Robertson and Lady.

"I'm sorry to keep you from work," the older woman said. "But I didn't hear from you last night and wanted to make sure you were okay."

The casserole was still on her table. Other things were on her mind besides eating. Now she contemplated on lying to spare her feelings.

"I apologize for that. I fell asleep and forgot to call you."

"That's all right, Susan. I am mainly concerned about you being by yourself. You should get a dog." Mrs. Robertson bent over and scooped the Poodle up in her arms. "Like Lady. Isn't that right, Lady?"

"Your concern is appreciated, but I assure you I'm fine."

"But there have been so many horrible things happening to young, single women nowadays." Distress engulfed her face and Susan had to say something to ease the woman's mind.

"I'll think about getting one." That seemed to help, and her usual smile bounced back in place.

Susan did not need a dog. Her parents paid for her to take either a gun or karate classes several years ago, and she chose the latter. Guns killed people and should someone attack her, she did not want to end their life. Just make them wish they were dead.

"Oh, before I forget, I have a skeleton key to all the apartments. So, if you forget yours or something, let me know. I do some housecleaning for the apartment manager sometimes, so she gave it to me.

"My, look at the time. I am keeping you from work. Scoot, girl, before you're late." Mrs. Robertson flapped her hands as if she were shooing a fly.

Susan laughed to herself but maintained a smile for the older woman. "Yes, ma'am. On my way."

The wind stirred up some fallen autumn leaves on the ground. Cold air blew across her chest, causing her to pull her jacket closer to her body.

The weather report said the day would be a chilly start. However, the day ahead of her would prove to be more chilling than the weather.

* * *

The drive to the store was not long enough to give her time to face the confrontation with Barbara about going to the auction. She decided to stay out of sight from both her boss and Craig by keeping busy dusting.

Heading down the aisle to the unicorn section distressed her seeing them but comforted her at the same time. Even though her sister was not there, the unicorns brought her to life in her mind.

Rose was three years younger than Susan and too trusting of other people. Prayerfully she had not trusted the wrong person. She vaguely remembered reading somewhere before about some people who worked in a bargain store getting busted using drugs. Susan was sure Rose would not be hooked up with people like that.

"Susan, I have been looking for you."

"Hi Barbara. Thought I would finish what I didn't get to yesterday."

"I like seeing your enthusiasm about finishing what you start. Not many people have that trait. But I would like to take a few minutes of your time if you don't mind."

Barbara's eyes, which were so brown they almost matched the color of her short black hair, had an innocent yet serious expression about them. Her grin was perfect, one that you had a hard time saying no to.

"Now?"

"Yes, now please." Barbara pointed toward her office, and Susan took off in that direction with her boss close behind.

Once inside, Susan sat in the chair in front of the desk. Barbara almost melted into the leather seat opposite of her.

"This is only your second day, but today we attend an auction. I like to introduce my new employees to this company in different ways. Make them feel part of it. And appreciate where they work at even more. Plus, they get an inside view at various jobs involved in this business. I would like for you to join us. It will take most of the day, and you will be compensated. I hope you will say yes."

Barbara made it sound as if she had a choice and would be able to turn her down without remorse.

"As you have said, this is my second day here. I'm still learning the store, and I would feel more comfortable if I stuck around here."

Susan felt confident in her decision. Barbara, however, had a long face. So much for not regretting turning her boss down.

"Well, I had hoped you would come. Some of my enthusiasm for you is a little early yet. If you prefer not to come, that is fine." She grimaced a bit as she finished the last sentence.

"Let me think it over. It might be the new job jitters. When were you planning on going?"

Barbara's face lit up. "In about an hour. I do hope you reconsider."

"I'll give you an answer by then," Susan said as she vacated her chair.

Once out of the office, she turned to go down the hallway and collided into Craig. He reached out and steadied her. His arms still held the strength in them she remembered. Chill bumps climbed up and down her body as the memory of him holding her the year before flashed through her mind.

The Stetson cologne danced with her perception. She wanted to bury her face into his chest and find comfort there but knew she had to stay at a distance.

"Are you alright, Miss Mullican?" Tenderness invaded his eyes.

"Yes. I'm fine." She caught hold of her wits and came out of his grasp.

"So, have you decided to go to the auction?" He raised his brows at her.

"No, I'm not going."

"Have you told Ms. Davis?"

"Yes. She gave me a choice."

"And you chose not to go?" His expression gave her the impression that she made a bad decision.

"Yes, why?"

Craig rubbed his forehead. "Come into my office, and let's talk."

Susan hesitated a little before following him.

Craig gently closed the door, then fixed his gaze on her.

"Do you really want to work here?"

What kind of question was that for him to ask her? Of course she did, but for reasons he would not know about.

"Yes," was all she said.

"The last person who turned Ms. Davis down she terminated soon afterwards. She perceived if they were not interested in learning the business, they were not interested in a career here."

"Now you tell me."

Craig held up his hands. "Hey, I tried to warn you last night. If you want the job here, I suggest you reconsider going."

"How can I be sure you're not bluffing me?" Worrisome hit her suddenly, forming a knot inside of her stomach. She did not want to lose this place of work, not until she found something out about her sister.

Craig hooked her chin with his finger and looked squarely in her eyes.

"I can't convince you to believe me. I can only tell you what I know. It is up to you to come up with a decision. Think about it, but don't think too long." He pressed his lips together, shifting his gaze from her eyes down to her mouth, and back up a couple of times.

She braced for a kiss from him, but instead he spun around and opened his office door for the two of them to exit. Then left her in the hallway to continue what he was doing before she bumped into him.

She stood dazed for a moment. The anticipation of his lips on hers and wanting him to embrace her still burned in her mind. But she knew that was not happening. Not now, or ever.

With that confirmed, she headed back to where she had been dusting. She had to decide about going to the auction. Fast.

Chapter 3

Did Craig tell Susan the truth about Barbara firing a person for not going to an auction? If an employee appeared disinterested in learning about the business that would be a good reason for her taking that action.

But why would he care if she got fired or not? What were his reasons for wanting her working there? So he could keep an eye on her like he said the day before?

She was not there to make trouble for him; she was looking for her sister. And if going to an auction helped her keep this job, then she would go. Besides, Barbara will be there with them.

She returned to her boss' office and told her she would be going after all.

"Excellent. I am glad you reconsidered. Give me about five minutes and I'll be ready." Barbara shoved some paperwork into a case.

Susan nodded, then proceeded out to the main area to wait for her. Craig was already out on the floor.

"So, are you going?" He flashed a sheepish grin.

"Yes, I am going, but because I didn't want to offend Barbara." That should slap the smugness off his face, not wanting to give him the satisfaction of knowing he persuaded her to go.

"I see."

Moments later Barbara joined them.

"Craig, you have everything we need?" Barbara's question was more like a statement.

"Yes ma'am. Ready when you are."

"Okay. Let's get this on the way." Barbara pulled her purse strap closer to her neck as she headed toward the door.

They approached the cosmetic counter when a voice came from behind them.

"Barbara. Barbara!" They turned to face a woman Susan had not met yet. She appeared to be about Barbara's age with light brown hair and dressed very sophisticated.

"Yes, Kathy. Is anything wrong?"

"I need to talk to you for a minute."

"I'll be right back," Barbara told them.

Kathy and Barbara departed. Craig spoke to Susan in a soft voice.

"She is Kathy Boyd, the owner's wife. Actually, she's more like the owner."

Her eyes caught sight of his mouth as he chuckled. Just the memory of being kissed by those lips took her breath away. She almost felt the tenderness and the urgency they held in a heated moment.

Linda, the bleached blonde cashier, appeared out of nowhere and stood between Susan and Craig. Her attention clearly focused on Craig.

"Craig," she began in a sultry voice, "can I speak to you for a moment?"

"Is it urgent?"

"Kinda. Do you mind talking over there?" Linda pointed in the direction of the jewelry counter, immediately taking off for it.

"I should be back before Mrs. Boyd finishes speaking to Ms. Davis," Craig told Susan as he followed Linda's lead.

Susan stood watching the pair as they talked to each other. They were far enough away that she could not make out what they were saying. It was not about business by the way Linda's eyes were star struck at him and messing with his collar.

Linda wore a leopard-print sheath with a plunging cowl neck displaying her cleavage in an enticing way. Craig took a couple of peeks at Linda's chest. Susan understood why, seeing how close she stood to him. After all he was a man, and they may be dating, reminding her not to involve herself with him again.

Linda squealed a "thank you" and gave him a big hug. After releasing him, she planted a kiss on his cheek.

On Craig's walk toward Susan, Linda's eyes twinkled with glee, and wearing a grin on her face. The smirk signaled Craig was Linda's--do not touch. Thankfully, a customer came up to the blonde taking her attention away from Susan.

Craig had a red outline in the shape of Linda's lips on his cheek. The temptation to let him run around with it on intrigued her, but her professionalism kicked in. Reaching around the cosmetic counter she presented him with a tissue. He gave her a quizzical expression, and she pointed to his face. Barbara came back to where they were standing as he finished rubbing off the rouge color.

"I'm sorry. Kathy has some problems I need to stay behind for. Do you two have any objections going on without me?"

Those words hit Susan like a ton of bricks. *Going on without me* echoed in her mind. Barbara's being at the auction was the reason why she felt less apprehensive about going in the first place. Her worst fears evolved, but how could she back out now? She hoped Craig would, but he seemed enthralled at the fact of Barbara not going.

"No, we don't mind. I will make sure I show Susan the ins and outs. You've taught me well in the six months I've been here how to pick and buy the items for the store."

A satisfied smile danced across Barbara's face when he said that. "I knew I could count on you. Now you two head on out if you are going to grab good seats. I will see you later. Don't worry, Susan. You're in good hands." She turned and left them alone.

"You heard the lady," Craig stated. "Let's go." Susan wanted to run and hide, but she had to go through with it now or face the possibility of losing her job.

The drive over was quiet. Nothing to talk about. Not wanting to discuss the past, and not much of a future with him, only work. And she surely would not tell him about Rose.

John Lancett told her not to let anyone know she was Rose's sister. It was hard with having the same last name. He had suggested she use another one, but she told him no. Some things she would keep under wrap, but she would not deceive people in that way.

Craig used two last names, Bryers and now Summers. But he had something to hide. Unfortunately, she found out what it was.

Craig worked at the More for Your Money store a couple weeks before her sister came up missing. Susan went to work there a month later trying to find out what happened to her. He did question her as to why the two of them had the same last name. She excused Rose off as being a distant relative and prodded him for what he knew about her. He was not extremely familiar with her, or so he said.

"Here we are. The front parking lot is full, so I had to park off to the side. Hope you don't mind walking a bit."

In an instant he had her door opened and held out his hand to her. "Shall we?"

She took it but tried to avoid getting too close to him. Warm feelings for him were creeping up, and she did not want to take a chance of more of them overriding her parameters.

* * *

Craig hated putting Barbara on the spot with Kathy Boyd. It would not take her long to figure out he had confused the payroll. But he wanted Susan alone, and uncover what she was up to. Other people having the upper hand made him uneasy.

He trusted John Lancett about as much as he did the devil. Not at all. When Lancett came to him a couple weeks ago wanting her hired on at the store, he sensed trouble. The only reason he agreed to it was because of the promise that she would be able to lead him to the person responsible for his wife's death two years earlier.

He could not understand how, or even why Susan would be mixed up with the Cartel. From his memories of her from last year, which tormented him frequently in his dreams, he could not envision her belonging to an organization as cruel as that one. There had to be some other way Lancett was associated with Susan, and he had to find the answer.

The auction house was crowded as usual, and he carefully guided her to the area where the items were shown. Taking out his phone, he started tapping on it.

"What are you doing?"

He raised his head from his typing to meet Susan's inquisitive eyes. "I'm inputting lot numbers of products which would sell in the store. You see these miniature colognes? People will pick these up fast. They search for bargains like this that are inexpensive and something they can use."

"Yes, but they're cheap ones." Susan crumpled her nose a little.

"Maybe, but you have to remember most of the people who shop there don't have an abundance of money. They can't afford the original Red like the one you're wearing."

He recognized the sweet scent she wore. Her disapproving face over the cheaper colognes showed him she had an expensive taste.

She had to have wealth from somewhere, also because of her high dollar clothing. He would find the answers one way or another about her involvement with the Cartel.

Susan blushed as she quickly excused off the perfume.

"It was a present from a friend."

"What type of a friend?"

Usually men gave women those kinds of gifts, and, reflecting back on their conversations before, he did not remember her mentioning any male friends.

Why would he care if a man did give her the perfume? Because of the feelings he still had for her darn it! Affections he needed to put aside for the sake of the case he was working on.

"A group of coworkers gave me a going away party from one of my jobs."

The answer she gave should not have mattered to him, but it did. Somehow jealousy crept into his being.

So much about Susan he did not know. She was secretive about herself. He was as well. But he had to keep his private life classified. At the first store he wanted to know her, but not as much as now. Now a desire in him to learn more about this woman came to life. That passion could prove to be dangerous. He had to be careful.

* * *

Susan was surprised and embarrassed at the fact Craig remembered which perfume she wore. He never asked how she acquired the expensive fragrance before, leaving her to wonder why he would ask now.

A unicorn carousel drew Susan's attention. She would buy it for Rose. Something to keep for her when, and prayerfully if, she found her.

She kept the unicorn's lot number in her mind. 947, which coincidentally was the same number her dad, Frank Mullican, put on his personal airplane. He named it Queenboat 947. The same one that crashed almost three years ago, killing him and his wife, Francis.

"Are you ready?"

Craig brought her gratefully away from her memories of her parents' death. She had been carrying around the guilt of the plane crash being her fault since that dreadful day.

"Yes. I hope you don't mind if I do some bidding of my own."

"Found something, did you?" He raised his brows at her.

"Yes, I did. Something for my sister." She stopped herself before she said too much about Rose. That was close.

"Five minutes until the bidding starts," the voice echoed over the speakers.

"Time to go, sugar." His smile made her want to melt. She had not been called by that name in a long time.

He placed his hand on the small of her back, directing her into the auction gallery. An electrical current ran through her body from the touch of his hand. Every nerve tried to reach out to him. She had to calm down and closed the front of her jacket covering the effect he had on her.

The man standing at the door handed her and Craig each a paddle, then they found a couple of seats towards the front. A few noisy minutes passed before the bidding started. The quietness overrode the room, except for the auctioneer, as paddles went up and down all around the place. Craig bid on specific items. Won some, lost some.

The auctioneer announced the bidding on lot number 947. Susan raised her paddle at ten dollars. There were other bidders. Thirty-five, and her paddle went up. More bidders came into play. Fifty, she raised again. She could not go much higher, not wanting Craig to know she had that much money to throw around.

"Do I hear fifty-five dollars? Fifty-five going once, twice, sold to the bidder for fifty." He laid his gavel down to close the bid.

"Yes. Thank you, God," she said half to herself, half aloud while letting out a sigh of relief. She looked over at Craig as he sat smiling at her, more amused than anything.

"I'm glad you won," he whispered to her, patting her leg.

"For the last item of the day we have this lovely case containing some unique shells found on the Florida beaches. We will start the bidding at five dollars."

Craig first raised his paddle. She concluded he was after the shells for Linda. The thought of him and Linda together distressed her, but it also helped to keep herself focused on finding Rose, and not cloud her mind with thoughts of him. Linda was the rope she needed to pull him out of her heart...this time.

Why did she think about him anyway? Their last time together over a year ago was getting too intimate. She should not have kissed him the way she did that day in his office. Nor should she have responded to his kiss with such eagerness.

To keep from feeling ashamed for the way she behaved that day she reminded herself she was human. It was natural to respond to a kiss and enjoy it when they were evidently enjoying it themselves.

She heated up from remembering the tingling sensation that kept building up to a point where she thought she would have exploded that day.

Bang! The sound startled her, bringing her back to the auction warm and thirsty. Automatically she fanned her face with her paddle.

"Sold to the bidder for twenty-five dollars." The auctioneer directed his gavel in Craig's direction. He had the last bid. A manner of satisfaction crossed his face, and she wondered if it was because of obtaining the shells for Linda, or the actual game of winning.

In any case she was glad the auctioning was over, and ready to get out of there and back to looking for her sister. If only it was that simple.

Chapter 4

Craig arranged for the items he bought for the store to be delivered there. They picked up Susan's carousel she won the bid on and deposited it into the trunk of Craig's car.

"I don't know about you, Miss Mullican, but the time spent in the auction house gave my stomach ample time to grovel for food." Craig patted his solid midriff.

"Shouldn't we go back to work? I'm sure Barbara is expecting us." She did not want to spend any more time with him than necessary. Especially alone.

With one smooth move he wrapped his arm around her waist and directed her toward a café across the street. "Don't worry, sugar. Lunch afterwards is always required. This place has some of the best hamburgers this side of Texas." The corners of his mouth turned up.

Inside the crowded café the dark wood lined the interior walls, along with the antique-looking tables and chairs. The electric lantern lights on a round wooden assembly hanged low with chains from the ceiling.

Susan and Craig were shown to a small table with two seats on the second level of the three-tier flooring and handed menus. Close by sat a water fountain with the appearance of days gone by with some coins in it.

The setting of the café gave off a mystical air. An impressive place to go for a romantic dinner, Susan thought, but they were far from being amorous again.

"So, what do you think? Kind of takes you back to the medieval times. I find this restaurant rather relaxing myself."

His eyes twinkled in the dim lighting. The scene fitted him well. His mustache, thin but masculine, and his dark features against the white shirt he wore reminded her of one of the characters out of that era.

"Are you ready to order?" The waiter drew her attention from Craig for a split-second.

"Yes, I do believe we will indulge ourselves in your famous hamburgers and fries." Glancing at Susan, she nodded her head in agreement. "To drink, I think one of your ginger-ales will do the trick." Craig handed the menu to the server.

"Same here," she said following suit.

Susan analyzed how sure he was of himself. Even to ordering food. Was he as sure of her keeping his little secret back at the first store? Did his deceit have anything to do with Rose disappearing? She would be cordial to him, but only to see what she could draw out of him.

"This is an enchanting place," she told Craig, giving him her approval. "I like it."

"I'm glad you do." The tone in his voice told her other things were on his mind.

"Tell me, Miss Mullican, what made you decide to come to work at The Five and Dime Store?"

"Oh, you know how it goes. You lose one job; you go hunting for another one."

"Yes, but it's about a hundred miles away from the one we worked at over a year ago. What brought you out this far south?"

"Just needed a change. It was getting dull back in the city. A small town seemed to be more suitable for me."

"Why in this direction? Why not further east?"

"That was not where I wanted to go. I could turn these questions around and ask you the same." He gave her the leeway she needed to find out some things for herself.

"Yes, and I would tell you my family is here."

Family? He never spoke about relatives before. Then she remembered he was leading a double life. Was his last name Bryers, the one he used at the first store? Or Summers, the one he goes by now?

"I think," he started as he reached across and toyed with a strand of her hair dangling lazily down her blouse, "you might be following me?" His eyes met her gaze.

"Following you? What do you mean? And what benefit would I receive from doing that?" She straightened up in her chair, causing the lock to slide out of his hand, giving him a dirty look.

He clasped his hands together on the table, setting his lips firm before speaking.

"You need to look at it from my point of view, Miss Mullican. We both worked at the More for Your Money store. You broke into my office, and I let you go. Here we are a year later and about a hundred miles away, and you show up. Now how coincidental is that?" He eyed her with a hard stare.

It was not exactly as he said. Yes, she did go in there while he was out, but he did not just let her go. A very audible threat came with dismissing her.

"Craig, why would I come around you after our last encounter at that store? I have better things to do with my life than to chase you around the world."

"Oh." He raised his brow. "Like what?"

"None of your business."

Drawing his hands towards himself, he gave her a smirk. "We'll see."

"Your hamburgers," the waiter said as he put down the plates in front of them.

They kept silent the remainder of the meal. After thinking for a while, Susan understood why he would think she was following him. She had not given him a good reason for being there since she could have worked anywhere.

No matter how intent he was with his questions, or changed his tactics and tried to charm her, she would not tell him. It would be hard to resist his charisma. She considered him good-looking with a decent personality when he was not being pushy.

* * *

From across the table Craig watched Susan, trying to figure out how to access that head of hers and find out why she was there. Plus how she could lead him to the person responsible for his wife's death, as Lancett foretold.

When she tried turning the questions around, he surprised himself by his answer. He did not really have family members there, but he did consider most of the people in his unit brothers and sisters.

She played it cool, acting as if she did not know what he was talking about. Then telling him it was none of his business for her being there, along with sticking that stubborn chin out at him. Susan had been headstrong ever since the day he met her. She was not going to give anything up willingly. He would play up to her, befriend her.

"I apologize for accusing you of following me. I guess it seemed too much like a coincidence that you are here at the same place as I am. I hope you can understand." He clasped his hands together under his chin resting his elbows on the table.

Susan leaned toward him, with her face close to his.

"Craig, it's unfortunate you think I'm following you, because I'm not. There is no reason to. Since we are questioning about each other, I would like to ask why you changed your last name?"

He wondered when that question would pop up and had rehearsed in his mind several times the answer he would give.

Reaching out he lightly ran his index finger down the side of her face, starting from her temple, and ending underneath her chin. His eyes followed the route his finger took. Focused on Susan's eyes, he pulled her tenderly to him, bringing their lips inches away from each other's.

"I can't tell you why I used two last names. I can only tell you the reason is job related. The best thing you can do is remember my last name now is Summers, and not to tell anyone about Bryers. Is that understood?"

"Yes, but what is your real last name?"

"Does it matter?"

"Well, I, guess not now. Might have if we continued on with our relationship."

He had wondered before what life would have been like if they furthered their friendship, but objects were in their way. He had to keep himself centered on his reason for being at the store.

"We didn't, and aren't now, so don't worry, and keep your nose clear of where it doesn't belong." He gave her a quick, tender kiss on the lips before removing his hand from her chin.

* * *

She sat back in her chair, taking in his last words. She knew they were not going to continue with their relationship, but to hear him say that had set it in stone.

But if he was serious about it, why kiss her? Why bring back those warm and passionate emotions she once enjoyed with him? Those feelings she had not experienced with anyone, including her one and only boyfriend back in Louisiana.

* * *

The walk to the car was just as quiet as the area. It was a Saturday afternoon and hardly any cars left in the parking lot. The only people around were a couple in passing and a jogger.

Craig was unlocking the passenger side when Susan felt a clammy hand grab her mouth, pulling her to a solid body. Cold steel shocked her temple, freezing her vocal cords.

Chapter 5

The assailant remained quiet as he held one hand over Susan's mouth and a gun barrel against her head with the other. Craig's back was to them while he opened the car door for her. He turned around, and his expression quickly went from pleasant to agitated. Craig immediately reached behind him.

"I don't think so. The only thing I want you retrieving is your wallet. Now hand it over, or she gets it."

The man pulled Susan closer to him, keeping the weapon to her head. The odor emanating from him reminded her of an unbathed transient who came into the E.R. while she was in training.

Oh, no! Was this what it was like before you die? Not only visual flash backs, but odors too? She was not ready to take her last breath yet.

The gunman, evidently proud of his position in this situation, was still rambling on.

"I'm sure you wouldn't want anything to happen to this pretty lady here." He kissed her hair, infuriating her even more. Craig's irises turned an eerie black color.

Susan had taken karate classes several years ago, but no reason to use the moves... until now. She prayed she would be able to remember them, waiting for the right moment.

"Come on, man. I don't have all day here." The man waved the gun around.

Now, she thought. She stomped on the man's foot. He slackened his hold a bit. She elbowed him in the gut, but he was too close to her. The force behind her elbow was not enough for the action to have an impact, other than bending them both over at the waist.

A gunshot rang out. The man jerked upwards as he released his grasp on her, and the sound of him running away echoed in her head.

She did not know who shot at whom until she raised back up and found herself looking down the barrel of Craig's gun. Chills crept through her body.

Craig cursed through his clenched teeth. In two swift steps he was in front of Susan, pulling her trembling body to him. He held her firmly and gently kissed her hair. She invited the warmth and protection she felt there in his arms.

He moved her away from him checking her over. "Are you going to be alright?" His irises were coming back to the golden color, but pain and anguish remained in them.

"Yes. Are you going to chase him?" Her words were a little shaky.

"No. I am going to call it in to the police station. He's left a trail of blood, so he won't be too hard to find."

"Blood? You, you shot him?"

"Yes, but don't worry. I only wounded him in the arm. He'll be fine, as far as his arm goes." Bitterness hit in his last words. She was afraid to think about what Craig might do if he ran across that man again.

He sat her down in the passenger's seat. "I'll be right out here making the call." She closed the door and watched in the side mirror as he put the phone to his ear and rubbed the back of his neck with his free hand.

Craig shooting a man holding her brought questions to her mind. What was he doing with a gun? A concealed one at that. Would an accountant need to carry one? They would if they were laundering money. Those books she found at the first store proved to her he was up to no good.

Flashing lights caught her attention. She observed in the side mirror two police cars pulling up behind them, then the officers approaching Craig.

Craig's BMW kept out noise, so she could not hear what they were saying, but she had the impression he knew them. They stepped out of her view.

After a few moments Craig appeared, taking his seat on the driver's side.

"The law will take it from here. I am going to take you home and let Ms. Davis know what happened. I'm sure she won't mind if you take the rest of the day off."

"What about my car? It's still at the store."

"I'll bring it to you."

"What about the police? Do they need me to make a statement? And take his fingerprints off me to find the creep?" She grimaced at the thought of the gunman touching her, and hastily wrenched out of her jacket throwing it in the back seat.

"They don't need any prints off you. When you hit him in the gut, he dropped his gun. As far as a statement goes, I persuaded them to let you give it later."

Susan did not want to ask how he got her out of the questioning. At that point she was glad he had. She was drained emotionally and physically and wanted to go home.

They pulled up to the apartment complex, and she guided him to her parking spot. She promptly exited the car before he made it around to her side.

"I appreciate you bringing me home. I'll just take my item I bought from the auction and go on in."

"Are you sure you're going to be okay?" He rubbed her arms up and down, causing a warm sensation.

She wanted to collapse on to his chest and be comforted there but decided not to. She was having a hard time trusting her feelings. Despite the fact he saved her from the attacker, the gun Craig carried terrified her worse.

For now, she wanted to put some distance between them, and moved toward the back of the car, leaving him standing there.

"Yes, I will be fine."

In a few strides he positioned himself at the trunk. Bringing out her carousel, he held it up, admiring the unicorns. His golden eyes flashed with amusement as pure pleasure danced on his lips.

"This is definitely a treasure." He handed it to her with care. "I used to have one of these when I was younger."

"Do you collect unicorns?"

"A long time ago. My father said only girls collected them, so my mom gave them away to a second-hand store. My favorite was a unicorn lamp with a light stuck out of its head."

All too clearly Rose's room flooded back into Susan's memory as she felt the tears building up again. Her emotions must have been easy to read because Craig asked her if he said something wrong.

"No. My sister had one. That was her favorite. I need to go and take a shower."

His expression turned remorseful and nodded in agreement.

"Before I forget I need your key to your car."

Susan took a key off her ring and handed it to him.

"I'll bring it to you later and check on you."

"That's fine. Talk to you then."

She hurried toward the door, making sure he did not attempt to touch her again. In her weaken emotional state she could not trust herself not to fall apart in his arms.

On her way to the shower her phone rang. She was tempted to ignore it, but in case it was John calling, she decided to answer it.

"Hello," she said into the receiver.

"Hi, Susan. Is everything okay?"

Mrs. Robertson was on the other end, but she had no time for her at that moment.

"I'm fine. About to get in the shower, so I'll talk to you later."

"I couldn't help but to notice some gentleman bringing you home. Is your car in the shop?"

Susan wanted to scream her business was none of her concern. But she could not bring herself to be disrespectful to the woman who had been so kind to her since she had been there.

"You could say that. The man who brought me home will be bringing it back to me. Now I need to go."

"I'll talk to you later. Goodbye now."

Susan's head began to pound and grabbed a couple of aspirins from the cupboard along with a glass for some water. After a few moments of relaxing, she took in a deep breath. The odor still clung to her. Without hesitation she snatched some clothes from the bedroom, then headed for the bathroom.

The shower was refreshing as it washed away the day. She closed her eyes then immersed her head under the cascading water.

Darkness invaded the room unexpectedly. Immediately she came out from under the water. Upon opening her eyes she detected a shadow of a man standing in front of her shower curtain.

Panic gripped her insides. Her breathing went shallow, causing her chest to hurt with each breath she took in. Had the attacker followed them to her apartment, and broken in?

She was on the verge of screaming when a familiar voice spoke up.

"It's me, Craig."

"What do you want?" She turned off the faucets and reached out for her towel. He placed the cloth in her searching hand.

What was he doing in her bathroom? Did she leave the door unlocked? She was unnerved by the gunman, but surely not enough to forget something that important.

She pulled back the shower curtain, pleased he had the courtesy to look the other direction while she had wrapped herself up in the towel. As he turned back towards her, he took a quick glance up and down her body.

"I brought you your car, and your jacket you left in my vehicle. I knocked, but no one answered. A sweet old woman with her dog came up to me asking what I was doing. After I told her, she let me in. I didn't mean to scare you."

"I'll have to talk to Mrs. Robertson about letting strangers in my apartment."

"I'm hardly a stranger. Her pooch, I believe she called her Lady, liked me. She said Lady licking my hand told her that I am a good guy. Plus, she gave me a thorough shake down before opening that door. Her seeing us together earlier when I dropped you off helped. You have a sincerely concerned neighbor watching out for you."

Susan had thought of Mrs. Robertson as a lonely nosy widow woman. In the couple of weeks she had known her, she started to feel the same way about the older woman as Craig did.

He was right when he said he was not a stranger. Susan knew some things about him. Like how soft his eyes were when he smiled a certain way. His gentle manner most of the time. The caring nature he displayed, especially when it came to kids. He had shown that at the first store when a little five-year old got separated from her mom. Craig helped the girl find her parent while soothing her anxiety of being lost.

There were also some things about him that she should not know. Like he could be involved in a criminal act.

"All right," she started. "Mrs. Robertson is cleared from allowing you into my apartment. But why didn't you call out my name?"

"I did a few times. When you did not answer, concern that the lunatic followed us here and forced his way in to finish the job had entered my mind.

"After stepping inside further, the sound of running water caught my attention and I walked toward the opened bathroom door. I waited for you to emerge from under the water to inform you I am here. Sorry to have startled you."

The openness of his explanation, and the look on his face, softened her heart toward him...some. She would still be careful around him.

"Thank you for bringing me my car, and my jacket. Now, if you don't mind, I need to get dressed. You can find your way out, the same way you came in. I will see you tomorrow." She backed him out of the bathroom and shut the door.

That was close, she thought to herself, her back against the door. What was she going to do with her feelings for him?

Her longing for the way life was before between her and Craig, and the strange air sitting between them now, caused some emotional turmoil for her. She would have to put those thoughts aside and concentrate on her main concern. Finding Rose. For now, she had not gotten anywhere.

* * *

Susan snuggled into the couch in front of the television. The phone rang. Presuming Craig was calling to check up on her, she tensed up a little. She wanted to talk to him, but her nerves were still a bit on edge from the incident with the attacker and the bathroom.

Not recognizing the number she answered anyway.

"Are you alright? After I heard what happened to my sweetie, I had to call you for myself."

Sweetie. It was John Lancett. He called her by that endearment. Disappointed it was not Craig, she nevertheless relaxed.

"It was nothing. How did you find out?"

"I have my sources," he chuckled. "Have to keep up with you. Don't want you looking for Rose alone. Just wish I could be there to help you, but you know how the office is."

"Not really. Remember I am the one who did not want anything to do with my parents' company. I am pleased you agreed to step in and take over the president's seat for me. Otherwise, the business would be in a mess, one you couldn't imagine."

"Possibly, but you still have the final say so in what happens with the corporation. On to other things. How is the search going? Find out anything about Rose yet?"

"No. Haven't been able to do much. Barbara had me go to an auction today, so I could not explore the store. Are you sure I can't ask someone there about her? Maybe bring her name up in a casual conversation?"

"No, Susan, you can't. Mike and I both told you putting that information out there could hurt Rose more than help her. You need to keep your eyes open. Don't be fooled by anything or anyone there, understand?"

"Of course. Am I looking for anything in particular?"

"Hard to say at this time. When I find out from Mike what we are supposed to be looking for, I'll let you know. Be safe."

"I will."

"It's very crucial, Susan. Don't want anything happening to you. Talk to you again before long." He hung up.

"Bye," she said to the dead phone. John never said good-bye. In a way he was a strange guy. He had been with her dad's company for ten years. While John was in college learning about the business, her father had hired him. She was barely a teenager then.

His looks were still the same as then. Soft brown hair. His eyes were the most striking blue. Almost piercing. And a prominent jaw line. He was a foot taller than her. He was no Craig--not that she wanted either man.

John had a skill for her parents' company. Strong willed for what he wanted. They had a couple of run-ins, but she usually won.

He had asked her a few times to marry him. As much as she liked him, she could not see herself doing that. After a failed relationship with her former boyfriend, she could never marry. Much less fall in love.

Craig was as close as any man would be since then. No matter how much Craig rocked her emotions, she would not allow herself to succumb to him.

Chapter 6

The sun shone down on Susan as she drove to work, uplifting her spirit. The day was a new one, and she was ready to continue her search for Rose.

As she entered the store, Barbara rushed over to her.

"Susan, how are you? Do you need another day off?" Concern for Susan's health was written on Barbara's face.

"I'm fine, thank you."

"Great. How about if today we have you pricing the merchandise? The items delivered from the auction are fantastic, but they will need to be marked for sale. I'll start you on it."

Susan followed her toward the back of the building. In a little area off to the side sat the boxes from the day before. Barbara opened the first box, which contained the colognes, and grabbed a pricing gun from a nearby shelf.

"I'm assuming you have used one of these." She held the gadget out. Susan nodded, and took hold of the instrument.

The contraption was the same at each store she had been in. She would rather be holding a stethoscope checking her patient's heartbeat instead. This was one of the sacrifices she willingly made to find her sister.

"The prices for each box are on this clipboard here." Barbara extracted a wooden board from the shelf the pricing gun was on. "Notify me when you're done. I'll be around." She handed the clipboard to Susan and walked away.

Exploring the store today was what she wanted to do. Now she was stuck putting prices on items in the back, away from the main action.

Resigning herself to her task, she started down the item list for the colognes. She noticed a couple of the boxes had the word HOLD beside it, but not for whom.

"Hey. How ya' doin'?" A young man in his late teens, early twenties came up to her. "You must be Susan. I'm Joey. I mainly work in the back, so you won't see much of me." He flashed a friendly expression, then held out his hand. While shaking his hand she noticed how flush his face was, and his hazel eyes appeared constricted between the squinting of his lids.

"So, Barb got you pricing these things, huh." He leaned against the wall raking his fingers through his stringy, dishwater blonde hair. "That's usually my job."

"If you'd rather do this, I'll give it to you." She held the pricing gun out to him.

He chuckled and straightened back up. "Na, you can keep it. I've got other things to do. See ya'." He picked out a key from the board beside the door which led to the back room, then proceeded through the doorway.

She studied the other keys. One of them had a paper tag with Craig's name on it, figuring it was to his office.

He was the accountant for this one also, and he had the paperwork on the employees. If Rose did in fact work there, Craig would be in possession of that information. She could sneak in and look through his files.

But what if she got caught? Would it be a repeat performance of what happened before? She did not want to risk losing her job, or worse, if he found her in there. The timing would need to be perfect for her to do it.

She continued with the pricing of the colognes. About midway through she heard something behind her and observed a teen-age boy slipping into the backroom. She shrugged it off as being one of Joey's friends.

After finishing one box, she took a break and walked around the store. She did not know what to search for but wanted to believe she was doing something to help find Rose. It was hard waiting on John and Mike to tell her what her next move would be.

Susan observed Barbara waiting on someone and noticed the emptiness of the place except for a few teenagers hanging around. They picked up items, commented on them, then placed them back in their spot. They were not interested in buying anything, only wasting time.

Scanning over the store she met Craig's eyes. She smiled then nodded at him. He returned it, then proceeded into his office. How long had he been observing her? He said he would keep his eyes on her.

Susan took a short trip to the restroom before picking back up where she left off at with the pricing, not wanting to give him any real reason to suspect her of snooping around.

She bumped into Linda when she came out of the room.

"Oh, hey. Did you check out the shells Craig got me at the auction?" Linda wore a broad smile.

Susan's memory went back to the day before when the auctioneer announced the ones from Florida, and he had instantly raised his paddle.

"No, I didn't, but I do remember him bidding on them." She was being polite to the other woman, even though she wanted to scratch her eyes out. Linda was a sly she devils, primarily when it came to Craig.

Linda carefully pulled something out of her front pocket in her white slacks. The shell was unique looking. Oval with brown stripes running lengthwise all the way around.

"That is nice," Susan complimented.

"Here, feel it." Linda's blue eyes were twinkling as she placed it into Susan's hand. It was smooth as glass.

"This was an impressive find, Linda. I never knew Florida had such beautiful shells."

"The funny thing about this particular one," Linda started as she retrieved the item from Susan and held it up. "This is an Amoria Zebra shell."

"I can understand where they arrive at that name. It does have the appearance of a zebra with its stripes. So, is it rare for Florida?"

"Yes. These are found in Queensland, Australia."

Susan was amazed at the knowledge her fellow worker had about shells. She asked her how she knew so much about them.

Linda's cheeks went rosy. "My parents used to take me to different beaches when I was growing up. They got me started in learning about them. I can't go anymore. So, every time Craig or Barbara goes to the auction house, I ask them to look for shells for me. I also go to other bargain stores checking for ones I don't already have."

The hunt reminded her of her little sister. She went to various places searching for unicorns. Susan decided to ask her some questions.

"How long have you worked here?"

Linda wrinkled her face. "Mm, about two years."

"Do they have a big turn over in help?"

"Not really. The lady before you came was here for about a month, I guess. I would call her Blondie. Funny cause we both are blondes. I think hers was natural though." A chuckle escaped Linda's lips.

Susan's interest peaked. "Do you remember her name?"

Linda wrinkled her face again. "No. We didn't work together very often."

Barbara came up to the two ladies. "Sorry to break up your chat, but we've got a business to run here." Her smile was pleasant as she drew Linda back to the floor.

Walking down the hallway she witnessed another teenager go through the back door. Now that was suspicious. She progressed to the door. Before opening it, an unknown deep and demanding voice came from behind her, startling her.

"Miss Mullican." An older man with graying hair walked toward her.

"You are Susan Mullican?"

"Yes, yes I am. You are?"

"I'm Jim Boyd. The owner of this store." He reached out shaking her hand, keeping a firm grip on it.

"I'd like to find out more about you. Come." He released her hand and guided her away from the door by her elbow, not giving her any leeway to move away from him.

They stopped at a doorway. After opening the door, he motioned his hand for her to go in first.

His office looked similar to the other ones. On the walls were documents and diplomas for business. A shelf at the back of the room held books on various subjects, along with a couple of family pictures. She recognized Kathy Boyd, but she did not spot any of children.

"Please be seated." She sat down in the chair indicated.

As he settled across from her, his appearance was fierce and organized. She hoped in this case looks were deceiving, because of the experiences she had with her father, and being systematic was one of his characteristics. Frank Mullican would be ruthless with questions when he wanted to find something out, especially if something did not fit in his logical order.

"Are you pleased with your position here?"

"I have only been here for three days now. Yesterday does not count since I went to the auction house. But so far I like it."

"True about your time here. I read in your paperwork your last employment was about a hundred miles away. So, what brings you to this particular outlet?" Jim clasped his hands together on the desk. His smile was more businesslike than personal.

"A friend told me about The Five and Dime Store. Said it would be a good place to work at."

He leaned over, gazing firmly into her eyes. The green hues in his irises reminded her of those belonging to a cat that would fluff you up for its own purpose, while using its claws to dig into you.

"Who is your friend? Maybe I know him or her."

Not willing to give out John Lancett's name, but against John's advice, she was going to use the owner of the store to find out about her sister. She took in a deep breath, and a leap of faith.

"Rose Mullican. She is also a distant relative of mine. Are you familiar with her?"

His eyes lit up as he sat back in his chair. Before he answered, a lady rushed in holding a newspaper. It was Kathy Boyd.

"Jim, did you see this? It is ludicrous! How could they say things like that about discount stores running dr...?" She stopped before finishing her sentence.

Susan fixed her gaze from Kathy back over to Jim and visualized horns coming out of his head. His face stood motionless, and very eerie. His jaws bulged out from his teeth being clenched so hard she thought they would shatter.

Kathy turned in Susan's direction. Color drained out of her face from either fear, or embarrassment. Susan took the first to be true. The swift change in Jim's appearance and the surrounding atmosphere had her heart skipping a beat or two.

"This is Susan Mullican." Jim spoke up through his still clenched teeth. "I'm sure she isn't interested in what the papers say. You can only believe some of it, isn't that right?" He shifted his glare to her. The intense expression he gave almost knocked the breath out of her.

"Yes, you're right, Mr. Boyd." She squeezed those words through her now tightened throat.

"If you're done with me, I'll go back to my work." Fear replaced the uncomfortable feeling she had around him. She had to leave. Away from that room. Away from him.

"I'll get back with you, Miss Mullican."

Susan quickly vacated her chair and hastened out of the room. Upon closing the door, Jim vocalized his feelings about Kathy coming into his office without knocking and blurting out things she did not need to be announcing to everyone. She made a mental note to buy a paper and research what set him off.

By the countenance on his face when she mentioned Rose's name, Jim apparently knew something important about her. Now to find out what that something was, and her whereabouts.

After a few deep breaths, she walked back to her workstation. Another teenager slipped through the back door. Joey showed signs of drug use, formulating a hunch he was dealing drugs in the back.

Craig kept altered ledgers at the More for Your Money store for some reason. The thought crossed her mind before it had something to do with narcotics. Susan had to make it into the backroom to investigate, even if it did not lead her to Rose.

She looked around making sure no one stopped her from slipping through that door this time.

Chapter 7

Susan quietly closed the door after entering the back room of the store. As soon as she let go of the doorknob, someone grabbed her wrist and whirled her around, shoving her into a small room. Her assailant put both of her hands in a hold above her head.

"What are you doing back here?" Venom seethed out of the muffled voice. She gathered all her breath to scream. Before she could let it out, the attacker crushed her mouth with his.

The person muttered something while their lips were still interlocked. Her eyes adjusted to the dimness of the room allowing her to recognize who held her. Craig.

She tried wiggling her way out of his hold to no avail.

He moved his lips from hers, but still close enough his breath caressed her face as he continued in a soft tone.

"As I said before, what are you doing back here?"

The feel of his chest moving in and out as he spoke, made her all too aware of the firmness his body held. Along with the musk aroma lingering around him, getting lost in him would not be hard to do.

"Answer me." The low sternness in his voice alarmed her back into reality.

She kept her voice down as well. "I witnessed some kids sneaking in here. I wanted to see what was going on."

"You don't need to be back here at all. Is that understood?"

When she did not respond to him right away, he pushed himself more into her, if at all possible.

"Is it understood?"

Groaning with pain, she answered him. "Yes. Now get off me. You're hurting me."

He hesitated for a moment, then let off a little. With the possession of her hands above her head, he bent down and kissed her gently.

"I'm sorry I hurt you. I don't want you mixed up in what's going on back here."

Susan was caught off guard by this sudden show of affection.

"What is going on?" Even though he still detained her, she felt empowered with him confessing something was happening in the back room.

He scowled at her, squinting his eyes. "You're not in a position to ask me that question. I would strongly suggest you do not come back here again. Promise me you won't. Please." His tone softened back up.

She decided to succumb to him...for now. "I promise."

He let go of her. "I'm sorry."

Tenderly he stroked her face. Craig apologizing to her helped sooth the pain, but it confused her feelings even more.

He leaned over and kissed her forehead, then commanded her to leave. She started to protest, but he placed his finger to her lips and pointed for her to go. Reluctantly she did.

* * *

Susan proved to be harder to handle than he had first thought. Stubborn to an extent. Her hazel eyes were hard to read at times. He hated being harsh on her, but sometimes she gave him no choice. He had to make her understand the danger she was in if she did not already know. She still could be part of the drug Cartel.

Her coming to the back room put his assignment in jeopardy. He had been trying to figure out where she fitted in. If he had not been assured that she was a key to finding the man responsible for his wife's death, he would have turned her down for the job.

Still inside the closet composing himself before exiting, he became aware of the back door opening and closing again. He immediately came out thinking Susan had come back.

Jim Boyd stood at the door, surveying Craig up and down. He asked why he was in the room.

"Looking for something." Craig did not feel the need to tell him about Susan being in the back.

In the six months of working at the store, he caught wind of a few mishaps to the unsuspecting ones who found themselves on the wrong side of Mr. Boyd. He wanted to protect her from any harm that would come her way. Above all else from people who were notably dangerous, like Boyd.

"I spotted Miss Mullican lurking about here earlier." Jim's smile grimaced. "I don't want her stumbling upon what's going on back here. Any reason for employing her?"

Craig had no intentions of her discovering the drug dealing either. He was close to getting all the evidence he needed to shut down the operation. If she stepped into it now, it could hinder his investigation.

"We had an opening, and she fit the position."

"Did she say how she became aware of this store?" Jim inquired for a reason, but Craig was not too eager to give out any information about her.

"No, she didn't mention it to me."

Jim twisted his lips for a moment. Placing his hand on Craig's shoulder, he continued.

"She stated Rose Mullican, whom she said is a distant relative, told her about us. Now I do not recall this Rose but learn what you can about her. Miss Mullican's here for some intention unknown to me, and I don't like that."

"Why do you think she would be here, other than needing a job?"

"Let's just say when I questioned her earlier in my office, she gave off some indications that told me otherwise. Find me the answers I'm looking for, Summers. I'd hate for any accidents to happen around here." He put a little squeeze on Craig's shoulder before removing his hand, then exited back through the door to the main store.

Boyd's accidents were everything but that. Which placed more pressure on him to either find out what Susan's purpose was there, or extricate her out, pronto.

Perhaps the key Susan held involved Rose Mullican. The name sounded familiar, but he could not place the face. Did she have relatives here she did not tell him about? She said something about having a sister, but not her sister's name. And a sibling would not be a distant relative.

Kenny was eight years younger than he. He was the pesky little brother you could not shake off from the bottom of your shoes. Always following Craig around, and getting into everything of his.

Soon after graduating from high school, Craig left home to go into the police academy. After finishing, he accepted a job which took him about fifty miles from his family. Whenever he would call, there had been concerns about Kenny's rebellious attitude, and going in his own direction.

He still remembered the devastating morning when his mom called and told him Kenny overdosed on heroin. Craig kicked his own butt then and now for not being the one he turned to instead of the drugs.

After some serious soul-searching, and counseling, he switched from being a petty theft officer to an undercover DEA specialist. He took more schooling, but in the end, when he catches Jeremy DeVore, the *scum* responsible for Kenny's drug addiction, it will all be worth it.

To think back on that day gave him a worse headache. He rubbed the back of his neck, trying to loosen the knot.

Craig would look into who Rose was, but not for Boyd. Mainly after he had seen him and DeVore talking the other day.

* * *

Susan continued with pricing the items. She expected to spot another teenager, and when she did, she would try to uncover what was going on in the back. It had to be something, or Craig would not have stopped her, warning her against going back there again.

John told her to look for suspicious activities, and that was definitely one. Uncertain if it had something to do with Rose or not, she would find out.

She reached for a box cutter on a shelf above her. It slipped down and landed behind the boxes. When she bent down to retrieve it, she overheard someone talking.

"Hey, man, I appreciate it." The tone belonged to a teen-age boy. Susan started to come out to quiz the boy, but a different person spoke.

"No problem. You know where to go when you want some more. Tell your friends. I can always get what ya need."

"Sounds cool," the teenager responded. "I've got plenty of connections interested."

"Alright. See ya." The second voice matched Joey by the phrase 'see ya'.

She did not want him to discover her. If he caught her spying on him, he might cause her to lose her job. She was not ready for that to happen.

The teenager passed by the boxes near her, but he had not seen her. When the door closed, she figured Joey went back into the back room. But as she stood, she was facing him. His eyes widened, then narrowed as his face turned red.

"What are you doing back there?" His words carried tension in them.

"I dropped the box cutter behind them and retrieved it. See." She held up the tool to confirm her story.

He nodded, and added, "How much did you hear?"

"About what?" Susan gave a quizzical expression.

"Yeah, that's what I thought. Keep it that way." He scoffed as he strutted away. A sigh of relief escaped her lips.

* * *

Thankfully, the day was over. At least for work. She was tired emotionally, physically, and mentally, and all she could think about was putting her feet up and relaxing. The rest of the day proved uneventful as far as finding out about Rose, and the going on in the backroom. The teenagers disappeared as suddenly as they had appeared.

She hustled to her apartment door to avoid Mrs. Robertson. She was too exhausted to hold a conversation with the woman. As luck would happen, the elderly woman was waiting. Her gray-haired friend traipsed across the way with her pooch in tow.

Lady ran to Susan and jumped up and down on her, barking furiously.

"Down, Lady! That is Susan." She switched her attention to Susan. "I'm sorry. I can't understand what's gotten into her. Ever since a guy came knocking on your door, she's been acting strange."

"Do you mean yesterday when you let Craig Summers into my apartment?" This issue had to come out into the opening.

Mrs. Robertson's cheeks turned a rosy red. "Oh no, dear. I do apologize for it, but I wouldn't have let him in if he had not shown me his proper I.D."

"What I.D. was that? His driver's license?"

"Oh, my goodness no. It would take more than that for me to open a door for someone, particularly when it was not their apartment. Another man came here today looking for you. Lady did not like him, but a real charming sort of man. Tall with brown hair, and some of the prettiest blue eyes I have seen on a man." Mrs. Robertson blushed again.

The description fitted John Lancett, but he said he would be too busy with the company to come there.

"Did he say who he was, or what he wanted?" She spoke above the dog's barking.

Mrs. Robertson pulled hard on Lady's leash, causing the pooch to yelp. "Stop it now!" With her master's command, Lady sat and replaced her barking with whimpering.

She spoke again to Susan in her meek tone. "No, I'm sorry. I asked him, but he just said he would get back to you."

"Thank you for telling me."

"Wished I could be of more help. I'll let you go. You look tired."

Mrs. Robertson talked to Lady as they walked away. Poor woman, she thought to herself while unlocking her door. It must be lonely to only have a dog to talk to, but at least she had someone. Susan's recent days of being with Craig, and not being able to be with him, showed her how alone she really was. It was a sacrifice she made to find her sister.

Susan closed off the rest of the world as she stepped into the small foyer. Walking into the living area, she tossed her Saturday's mail and newspaper on to the coffee table and sat down on the couch taking off her shoes. She stood and pulled her shirt out of the blue jean skirt. As she unbuttoned the last button on her blouse, a priority letter on top caught her attention.

She picked up the envelope and brought it into the dining room under the light making sure she read the sender's name right. John Lancett. Why would he write her unless he planned on coming there? And why didn't he tell her on the phone yesterday when he called? He might have been whom Mrs. Robertson confronted that morning.

A shadow moved across the envelope. Someone was behind her. Her heart raced as her breathing went shallow. It made sense to her, now, why Lady had been barking. She tried to warn Susan somebody was in her apartment.

Chapter 8

Susan waited for the intruder in her apartment to come closer to her before making her move. If it was the same gunman from the auction, she knew what her mistake had been when she tried to take him down the first time. This time she would succeed.

With all her strength she swung upwards with her elbow, catching the person in the chin with such force it knocked him down on to his back. She spun around and planted her heel on his chest. Looking down she recognized John Lancett's face dazed but smiling up at her.

"Its times like this I'm glad you took the karate classes over the gun. Just think, I would be getting shot at instead of a shot of you." He shifted his brows up and down.

His words made her dreadfully aware of her blouse flying open over him, and he could see up her skirt. She quickly removed her foot off him.

He sprang up from the floor, and looked her up and down, giving out a whistle. "I like your attire."

Susan could feel her cheeks getting hot, and immediately buttoned her shirt with trembling hands. *Darn her hands,* she thought. *And darn John.* Why was he there anyway?

"Well?" She peered at him.

"Well what?" he shrugged while plopping down on the couch.

"What are you doing here, and how did you get in?" She was very annoyed with him as she rounded the sofa. Mrs. Robertson had not let him in. She crossed her arms in front of her body while waiting on an answer.

"How I got in, my sweet lady, is a secret a master doesn't reveal. As for why, didn't you receive my letter?" He elevated a distinguished brow to her.

Susan's mind went back to the mail she had been holding when she discovered the shadow. His shadow.

"Yes, I did, and I was just about to open it when you scared the daylights out of me. Why didn't you wait until I was home, and knock on the door like everyone else?"

"Because I was not informed of your time of arrival, and I didn't want the appearance of staking out your place sitting in front of it in my car. Also, I like giving you the element of surprise to make sure you can handle yourself, considering what happened to you at the auction house."

At times John acted more like a big brother to her than someone trying to acquire her hand in marriage. Always eager to be informed if someone had hurt her, mainly if men did.

The pain of remembering the force her prom date had put on her to have sex with him, then dumping her on the side of the road to walk home when she had refused, returned.

It had taken John to draw it out of her. He had left her father's side at an important meeting to coax her to tell him. His concern for her well-being, along with a teen-age crush she had on him at that time, had made it easy for her to talk to him.

Later she found out her escort was killed in a gang fight.

"Well, since you're here, John, tell me your reason for your visit, so I don't have to bother with opening the letter."

"Ah yes, that's right. You do not like bothering with letters. Your mother used to complain how you wouldn't write home."

Squinting at him, she commented on what he said being a low blow.

"Sorry, but it's true. So, sweetie, are you going to be a good hostess, and offer your company some refreshment?" He gave her a crooked smile. "Or do you require me to tell you of the news with a parched throat?"

"What? You came into my apartment while I was not here. Why didn't you get your own drink?" Hostility held in her voice. She could not believe the audacity this man had to intrude in her home and demand her to wait on him hand and foot.

John waved his right hand. "I don't know where you keep that stuff at. Besides, I have only been here twenty or thirty minutes before you came home." He smirked at her.

Susan stomped off. His news must be important for him to travel over a hundred miles, she thought while stepping into the kitchen grabbing him a drink. Perhaps he had some information leading to Rose. Maybe he found her little sister.

Hastily she came back in handing him a glass of water. He looked at it as if though she offered him something foreign.

"I drive all this way and all you bestow upon me is water? Now where's the hospitality?"

"Water is healthier for you than the Scotch you prefer to drink."

"Most likely, but Scotch tastes better." His dimples emerged on his cheeks.

Despite being upset at him, she could not resist laughing at the boyish expression on his face. "Yes, but I don't keep that kind of stuff here."

"After looking around this place, I'm amazed you keep anything here. How do you live in this place?" John replied with arrogance in his voice. "By the way, you have some of the nosiest neighbors I have ever seen. That old *bat* and her mutt, which, by the way, tried to take my hand off, were rude to me."

"That bat and mutt, as you call them, are the nicest ones around here. You, Mr. High and Mighty, are the one who told me to rent a place like this." She burned the glare of death at him.

Shock was written on his face, which changed to a sympathetic expression. "My apologies. I did convey that to you. It must be really hard on you."

It had taken her awhile to adjust to it, but she had grown to like her little apartment. To hear someone talk about it in that way offended her.

"I survive fine in this place, thank you. Now, answer my question before I throw you out." The sternness in her voice told him she was not playing around anymore.

"All right, but first tell me. Did you find out anything at the store yet?"

Susan took a seat in the chair facing him.

"Well, it is kind of suspicious, I think. Barbara had me pricing items today toward the back of the building, and teenagers were sneaking into the back room. I believe they were involved in drugs."

"Oh." John's eyes showed interest in her story. "What did you do?"

"I tried to follow them, to find out if that is what they were doing. Mr. Boyd, the owner of the business, and Craig stopped me."

He leaned forward, and in a caring way took Susan's hand. He focused on her eyes.

"Tell me, did Craig harm you in any way?"

Her heart quickened as she thought back to her encounter with him earlier that day. He had been a little rough with her, but she did not want to tell John. He had not injured her physically, just her emotions.

"No, Craig didn't hurt me."

He squinted his eyes at her. "You know I can tell when you're lying."

Susan was stunned by his statement. He had told her that before, and, of course, she was not truthful to him then. She pulled her hands out of his and put them up in surrender.

"Alright. You are right. But he only alarmed me."

"How did he alarm you?" A vein popped out of his neck, startling Susan. She decided to tell him the truth, but she would skirt around the in-depth details.

"Well, when I got into the back room, he was there. I didn't expect him." She shrugged it off, hoping he would let it go.

"What did he do or say to you?" John kept pursuing the incident.

"He asked what I was doing in the back. I told him I was following a teenager." Silence followed for a few seconds before he probed her further.

"And?" His eyes flickered with curiosity.

"He told me not to come back there." His eyes were fixed on her, waiting for her to say more. "That is it. I promise." Susan raised her right hand.

A satisfied smile danced across John's face.

"Good. Not about him frightening you in any way, but that he did not hurt you. Also, what makes you think the teenagers were doing drugs?"

"The stocker's eyes were constricted, and his face was flushed."

"You can determine this after not being in the medical field for over a year?"

His words perplexed her. "What are you suggesting by that? Just because I have put my job as a nurse on hold to try to find my sister does not mean my expertise is as well. One of the important things school taught was to look for signs of narcotic use."

"I'm sorry, Susan. I should not question your knowledge of your profession. Tell me, how do you think this might have anything to do with Rose?"

Her eyes narrowed as she bit her bottom lip before speaking. "I can't be a hundred percent sure, but I'll bet drug dealing was going on at the first place, the More for Your Money Store, and they probably murdered her because she found out about it."

John looked at her for a minute in astonishment, then chuckled.

"Sweetie, you have been watching too many television shows. What in the world would make you think such a thing? Specially after Mike and I told you she was working at this outlet not too long ago?"

"On the grounds that Craig worked at the first store also, and I think he was laundering money for drugs."

"Is there proof of this?"

"No, I can only tell you what I observed."

Suddenly he livened up, now more interested in what she had to say. "What did you see?"

"I didn't think it was important before, but at the More for Your Money Store Craig had two sets of ledgers. One of them I am sure he was using for something illegal. Primarily after the way he acted when he caught me in them."

John sat for a minute, thinking before he spoke.

"Susan, I can't go by that."

"Why not?" She glared at him.

"Accountants are known for having more than one record. One for the store and one for the IRS."

"How did you determine he was an accountant? I didn't tell you that."

He shrugged his shoulders. "You said he had ledgers, and accountants use those. I think you are stressed out from searching for Rose. You should take some time off."

Susan roared. "Take some time off? And do what? Lose my mind over my sister being out there *somewhere* and not knowing what's happening to her?"

Abruptly she sprung up and sprinted across to the dining room, aggravated at John for laughing at her. She had to flee out of his presence. Would have order him to leave, but she lost her voice. It had pained her he did not believe in her.

She watched as he came to his feet and leisurely walked over to her. He tenderly held her shoulder with one hand and brushed his fingers through the auburn waves of her hair slowly with the other one. His eyes observing the path they took.

"Susan, you understand I love you, don't you?" He turned his attention to her eyes, searching out her feelings. Cupping her face in his palms, he continued on.

"I want you for my wife. I have for so long. Please say you will marry me. It would mean so much to me." He lowered his head and gave her a tender kiss on the mouth, then pursued a deeper one. His arms wrapped around her waist, clutching her close to him.

She backed out of his embrace. "John, I can't. I'm sorry, but now would not be a good time for me to think about marriage."

"It's Rose, isn't it? We will still search for her. That would never cease. I know how important she is to you, and her disappearance brought you down mentally." He reached out for her hands, holding them in his.

"Look at me, sweetie. She means a lot to me as well. I spent years with you and your family. In fact, you two are a part of me. This has not been easy on you. First your parents' plane crash, and then Rose. But I will not leave you. I'll always be here for you." Gently he brought Susan's hands to his lips and kissed them.

John thought she did not want to marry him because of the search for her sister, but she did not want anyone.

She broke the hand ties and walked over to the sofa sitting down on it.

"I don't want to hurt you, but it just wouldn't be right at this time."

He parked himself on the coffee table facing her.

"Are you saying when we find Rose, you'll marry me?" A twinkle danced into his blue eyes, along with a hopeful countenance on his face.

"No, I can't promise that, and you can't expect me to be able to make a decision like that now."

He frowned and thrust to his feet.

"Very well, Susan. I do have some news you will be interested in." Sarcasm hit in his last words. He traipsed around the couch, picking up the letter she dropped earlier. Hitting it in his hand, he went on.

"Craig, the accountant at the store, is in possession of some information about Rose in a blue folder. Mike Holmes needs it for the case. I want you to locate it and bring it to me. I'll carry it to Mr. Holmes."

"So, I was right about Craig having something to do with Rose's disappearance. Why do you want me to swipe it? Can't Mike obtain it from him? And are you sure he has this folder?" She turned her head to view him.

He bent over and looked fiercely into her eyes.

"Look, you want to find your sister, don't you?" She nodded in response.

"Don't ask any questions. You are better off not knowing. Just do it, Susan. Your sister's life depends on it."

Without warning, he drew her mouth to his and gave a demanding kiss. When he let go of her, her head spun, and he was gone, leaving her with a decision she did not want to make.

　　　　　　　

She wanted to be reunited with Rose desperately, but what would Craig do if he caught her in his office. Last time he had threatened her. This time she may not be as lucky.

Chapter 9

Craig deceived her. He knew about Rose, and yet he said nothing to her. What was in that folder he was holding? Did it have Rose's whereabouts? Why was she missing? What kind of danger could she be in?

Or could it be that she left home, and he was helping her little sister?

The day they had laid their parents to rest had been hard on them both. After everyone had departed, her and Rose held each other. Tears streamed down their faces. Rose tore away first.

"Susan, what will you do now?" Rose sucked back the weeping.

"What do you mean by that?"

"Well, your school is in Louisiana. Are you going back?"

Susan smoothed back Rose's shimmering blonde hair. "No. I am going to finish college here in Central Texas. I'll move into the house with you, and we can take care of ourselves." She gave Rose a reassuring smile.

"What happens if we get mad at each other?" Her innocent, sixteen-year-old eyes had been full of concern. Susan chuckled sadly.

"If one of us gets upset at the other, we discuss it. Remember how mom and dad taught us to talk things out?"

"Yeah, but sometimes it doesn't work."

Susan drew Rose into her, hugging her like a momma bear.

"We'll prevail through this. We have had some rough spots growing up, but we are all we have. I won't abandon you. I promise." She had kissed the top of Rose's head. Rose sat up and had held out her little finger.

"Let's do the pinkie shake. We both vow never to leave the other."

That was one thing Susan thought Rose would grow out of. However, her parents had babied her.

"All right." They had done the ritual, each vowing never to forsake the other.

They had their ups and downs those two years before Rose disappeared, but Rose took pinkie shakes seriously and would never go back on one. Rose did not flee from Susan. She had to be in terrible danger. Susan would find the folder John told her about. Before handing it over to him, she would look into it herself. It will be risky, but she could not and would not let her sister down.

* * *

Beep! Beep! Beep! Beep!

Susan rolled over and pushed the snooze button...again. In her mind she was trying to remember how many times she had hit it. She had lost count and decided to see what time it was.

"Six thirty! Oh, my gosh!" With less than an hour to dress for work, she swooped up some clothes and made a mad dash for the shower.

She took a hard look at herself in the door mirror. The light blue blouse kinda went with the geometric design skirt she slipped on. The triangle pockets in front had a hint of blue. Susan settled on it, grabbed a protein drink from the refrigerator, and took off.

Stationed at the counter, she spied Craig as he came in at his usual time. He glanced over in her direction while in flight to his office with his quirky smile of acknowledgment and the winking of his eye.

He had some items in his hand. She skimmed over them but did not see a blue folder.

All night she fretted over going into his office while he was not there, but she knew she had to. Only once had she done something like that when she and Rose had sneaked into their father's workplace at the house and had gotten caught. Susan had covered with a story of a lost charm bracelet. He had reprimanded them for being in there and had grounded them both for a week.

The grounding did not bother her too much. The confrontation she had with her father distressed her most. Especially when she was doing something wrong. Making up a lie was hard for her, because usually she would get caught.

Her nanny, Ms. Eddie, would always say that a tale was like a snake. Once it got hold of you, it would bite you in the butt.

* * *

The morning dragged until lunchtime, giving her plenty of time to devise a plan. She observed Craig carrying a briefcase and heading fast paced out the door. She prayed the folder would be in his office.

Susan looked out the front windows as Linda sidled up to Craig, stopping him. Susan could not see Craig's face, but Linda displayed a radiant smile as she talked to him. She straightened his shirt, and he nodded, apparently at a question she asked him. He then brushed her hands aside and took off in the direction of the parking lot.

The scene she witnessed surprisingly sparked up some jealousy.

She could not think about that now. He was keeping vital information about Rose from her. She had to keep her mind focused on finding her sister. Linda came in and took over for her, and Susan put her plan in motion.

She headed to the restroom, but instead diverted in the direction of the board which held the keys, making sure no one was in sight. All hopes she was correct about the keys going to the offices. Once she located Craig's and grabbed it, she proceeded to his room. It was the right one. She dropped the gold-colored metal in her pocket and slipped in, closing the door behind her.

Unlike Jim Boyd's office, Craig did not have family pictures adorning his shelves. She was suspicious of if he did have family here as he had said before at the café.

She hastened to the bookshelf and searched through the books and folders that were lined on the shelves for the blue folder. Found one, but there was nothing in there about Rose.

She turned around to investigate the desk. His date book was open. He had a meeting that afternoon and would not be back for a while. She breathed a little easier knowing she had more time to explore.

A red ledger was off to the side. She spotted another one and flipped both covers over to expose the first page. They had the same dates, but different amounts. He was doing it again!

John had told her accountants kept two books, but she had a hard time believing that after Craig's reaction to her at the first store. There was a lot more than what John said. The scandal was one she could not worry about now.

Focused back on the desk, she caught sight of a blue notebook. As she started to retrieve it from under some paperwork, she heard a key in the door. She dreadfully waited for it to open.

Faced with an incredibly surprised Craig, immediately his expression went to rage with his golden eyes turning black. The door slammed a little harder than usual. In two swift steps he strode to Susan.

"What in blazes are you doing in here?" He was struggling not to shout. The fiery darts coming out of his eyes hit her with such force she thought they would knock her down. Fear wedged in her throat. She swallowed hard and steadied her legs. What was she going to tell him?

"Why are you back so soon?" Diverting the question should give her time to think.

He grasped her shoulders, then shook her a bit. "That's not the issue here. Why are you in my office?"

She grimaced in pain. Craig let her go. She backed up, and he kept in step with her, ending up at the wall.

"You're not getting away from me without an answer this time, Miss Mullican." He put his hands up on the wall, encasing her there between them.

She stared dazed into his chest, trying to find something to say. His crisp white shirt engulfed with his cologne intoxicated her. She had to turn her attention away from his scent or go somewhere she did not dare to.

"I'm waiting for an answer." His voice was not as harsh as before. She ventured her eyes up to his, noticing the golden color coming back and the softening of his face. His lips were still firm, and not far from hers.

"I was looking for something."

"That was evident. What?" A muscle in his jaw twitched when he spoke.

"The other day when you brought me my car along with my jacket to the apartment, well my charm bracelet was in the pocket of my coat, and it must have fallen out. I can't find it at home, and I thought it might be in here." That was a lie, but the only thing she could come up with. The irony of being able to use this story again did not escape her, but would it work?

"Why didn't you ask me about the jewelry instead of sneaking into my office?"

"Well, have you seen it?" She gave him an innocent look.

He glared her down before removing his hands from the wall and placing them on his hips.

"No, I haven't. Are you sure you put it in your jacket?" He jeered at her, twisting his lips. He knew she was lying, but he could not prove it.

"I thought I did. I could be wrong. Guess I should go." She scurried around him before he had a chance to grab her.

"Aren't you forgetting something?" He turned to face her and held out his hand. She reached in her pocket and pulled out the key she took from the board earlier and placed it in his hand. Before she removed her hand, he clamped his down around hers. Tight. She gasped then looked up at him.

"If you think your lame excuse is acceptable, think again. I don't know why you were snooping around in my office, but I hope for your sake you have a good reason."

He loosened up his grip some, but still held on to her hand, waiting for a response. The warmth of his hand on hers was causing a stir inside, but not one that he would be aware of.

She had to come up with some excuse for being in his office. She could not tell him about the folder. Perhaps one of her questions could be answered.

"You're going to think it's silly."

He released his hold on her hand as he raised his left brow.

"I was looking for evidence of you and Linda dating each other."

He held a straight face as he asked what kind of proof.

"Oh, love notes, days written on your calendar for dates with her, stuff like that."

"I see. So, tell me why it would matter to you if I was dating Linda?" Amusement sailed across his face.

What did he want her to say? That she wanted to pick back up where they left off at before the incident at the first store? Wanted to be with him? That she loved him, and could not stand seeing him with someone else?

If she was truthful with herself, the first two were true. The third one, she would have to dig deeper down inside of her heart to find that answer.

"No particular reason why. I was simply curious, that's all. But it's your business, and I had no right to invade in your privacy," she blurted out as she slowly backed up toward the door. With that said she was hopeful that he would let it go.

"You're right. It is my affair. Even so, if you really want to know something, come here."

He motioned his finger for her to come closer to him. His golden eyes gleamed at her. She stopped backing up and cautiously approached him.

With care, he brushed aside her hair from her ear, inducing a wave of pulsating vibes shimmying their way down to every nerve ending in her body. He leaned toward her.

"I never have, nor will I ever date Linda." The feel of his breath on her ear as he whispered intensified the vibrations, causing her body to quiver.

He abruptly moved away and turned toward his desk and straightened up a stack of papers.

"I've got some work I need to do, and I'm sure your break is over.

We will forget about you coming into my office this time. But I better not catch you in it again." He half turned in her direction, then bid her good day.

* * *

Darn it! he thought as she left the room. He was sure he had himself under control with Susan. When she came up with the story of Linda and him dating, he figured it would be amusing to taunt her. He enjoyed watching her expressions and body movements.

In the end he had to let her go or do something he may regret later.

The phone rang, startling Craig, and he yanked the handset up.

"Five and Dime Store. May I help you?"

"Yes. Craig Summers?"

"This is he." In an instant he recognized the voice on the other end of the line. He was one caller he had not expected to hear from and did not particularly want to talk to at that moment.

That well-known knot, becoming more frequent, hit the back of his neck. He rubbed his collar bone, trying to message the ache out.

Chapter 10

Susan grumbled to herself. Forget about going into his office? How could she? Craig had to be leading her on, playing with her. Well, he might not be seeing Linda, but he sure as heck was not going to see her either.

Apart from that, he possessed information about Rose she needed. That folder would have been found if he had not walked in on her. She would have to call John and let him know she did not get it.

Looking down at her watch, she had a couple of minutes before coming off-break. Quickly she picked up a nearby phone.

"Susan?" she recognized the voice on the other end. How odd that John was calling her at the store. Before answering back, she heard an all too familiar voice speaking.

"No, nothing else has happened to her. She is getting too dangerously close. Why is she here?" The demanding voice belonged to Craig. Why would he talk to John about her?

"Patience, my friend. Just keep her safe, no matter what. Oh, by the way, did you read yesterday's newspaper?"

"No. Why?"

"I'd suggest you do." John hung up, followed by Craig.

Susan was stunned. What was going on? What was she getting close to? Did it have anything to do with Rose? The store? Or her parents' company?

What about the paper? Could he be talking about the same article as Kathy when she rushed into Jim's office the day before? She had bought one but did not read it yet. A headache was coming on, and her stomach tightened.

"Please hang up and try your call later." A woman's voice cracked over the phone. The message started to repeat itself before she hung up.

Half stumbling out of the cubbyhole, she hardly detected Barbara asking if she needed help.

"You don't look well, Susan. You should go home and rest." Barbara's brown eyes filled with deep concern. She put a hand on Susan's shoulder to balance her. "I'll drive you if you want."

"No, I'll be fine. I'll just sit down for a bit." She gave Barbara a reassuring smile.

"All right, but straight home afterwards. No detours. Understand?" Susan nodded and did as she was told.

* * *

After the phone call, Craig glanced around. His ledgers were moved. He wondered how long Susan had been in there before his cancelled meeting brought him back. And how much she discovered.

He continued looking more on his desk and noticed an unfamiliar blue folder. He picked it up, opened and read the top page. It was titled 'The Rose'.

"How interesting," he mused to himself as he pulled up a chair, making himself comfortable. He flipped the sheet. It stated that the Rose had been missing since the ninth of May, over a year ago.

There was an account in a different book he kept for himself dealing with the businesses of the Cartel for a Rose.

He ensured his office door was locked, then advanced to the bookshelf. After moving some books aside, he removed the false wall inset which held another accountant ledger. He traced the account back to the same date.

He had a hunch it was a person's name. Possibly Rose Mullican, the one who Boyd said Susan mentioned as being a distant relative. The name sounded familiar, but not quite sure where, or if she was the one spoken of in the folder.

He started at the More for Your Money Store a few weeks before that date. Visualizing the names on the checks, he remembered a Rose Mullican.

"That's it!" He banged his fist on the desk. She was the distant relative Susan talked about before. Or could she be Susan's mysterious sister for whom she had bought the unicorn carousel.

The name now had a face. Rose was there for a short time, and he thought she had quit. He had not recalled any news about her disappearing in the papers, or on the television. Holmes, the detective in the missing persons' division, had not mentioned anything about a local from the store vanishing. But why would Susan keep quiet about her sister missing?

Some things about Rose came back to his memory. She was in her late teens. Spunky. Shimmering blonde hair. Eyes that always sparkled. Plus a bubbly personality.

Susan started working a couple of months after Rose left and the two of them being related had escaped him. He had a hard time putting his heart back into his job after grieving over his wife's death a year earlier. In spite of this he managed to notice Susan, which happened due to an accident.

He had been looking down reading some paperwork while walking, and his elbow hit a glass swan. It fell to the floor, shattering into a hundred pieces. He put his papers down to scoop it up. Susan had his hand bundled into a white towel, holding his arm up in an erect position before he realized he had cut himself.

He looked at the white cloth dotted with red, then at her. While her eyes were intent on his wound, he had taken the time to examine the woman with his hand in hers.

Her auburn hair neatly tucked back in a bow, except for a few strands that made their way out. Her hazel eyes glistened in his direction as she turned her head. She smiled so sweetly with inviting lips.

He tasted of those lips later, but they did not go any further than a few passionate kisses. She kindled a fire in the bottom of his soul. Brought out a desire for life in him again.

He still longed for her and finding it hard to keep his hands off her. Every encounter lately had been a test and he had to maintain his distance. The best thing for him was to keep focused on this case and off her. Besides, she more than likely hated him for threatening her before. And rightfully so.

After she discovered his books at the first store, he flew off the handle. He could not risk her finding out what he was doing. That would have blown his cover. Something he was not willing to chance.

He accused her of being a spy for the Cartel. When Lancett came to him wanting him to hire her, he knew she had to be one.

With the information he found on Rose, he prayed Susan was only looking for her. Even back at the other store.

He read on, and it mentioned the town Port Emerald. On another page a reference to Queenboat 947 was being used to transport the Rose. Had to be the name of the boat she was on, considering Port Emerald was on the bay. Near that vicinity was Summersville, a small boating community, where he spent his vacations with his aunt and uncle.

They both died a few years ago, and he had not visited the place since. He paid a couple to keep the two houses up that they owned and willed to him. It would be nice to go back, but he would have to make a choice. Should he continue his search for the man responsible for his wife's death? Or go on to find Rose who may still be alive and in need of help?

What would his father, Lt. Roger Summers, done in a situation like this? Would he abandoned one mission to work on another? If he remembered his story right, his father had. That is how he met Craig's golden eyed mother, Cecilia Hill.

Changing cases was something he would have to seriously consider, and ultimately approach his supervisor. Lt. Dan Johnson had an aversion to switching plans when the pieces were falling together. He would most likely advise Craig to turn the folder over to the authorities there, and have

Susan talk to them.

Strange to him, though, that it showed up on his desk. Perhaps this was the key he needed. Should he decide to find Rose, he only prayed he would not wind up as a target for the drug Cartel. He would have to keep his guard up.

* * *

The phone conversation Susan overheard between Craig and John still had her dumb founded. She could not understand why they were talking to each other, and their intentions. And which one should she ask about the communication between the two?

So many questions and no answers. She decided on a quick shower to help wash away some apprehension concerning the two men and her sister. She needed to clear her head.

Afterwards, she threw on a robe and plopped down on the couch melting into its cushions. On the coffee table sat the newspaper from the day before. She picked it up and skimmed through the headlines.

'Close-out Stores Dealing More Than Knickknacks.'

"That must be it," she uttered to herself, wondering if this was also what John referred to.

She read on. The article implied teenagers ran drugs through the outlets. Likely the reason why Joey and his friends went into the back. Was that what Jim Boyd and Craig tried to keep her from seeing?

The paper named some businesses closed down because of the drug dealing. The More for Your Money Store, the first retailer she worked at, was among them.

Her hunch was right about Craig. He was laundering money. Now he was doing it at The Five and Dime Store.

The report brought on a worse headache than the phone conversation she eavesdropped on. She downed a couple of aspirins, then laid on the sofa, falling fast into a deep sleep. Nightmares invaded her dreams.

There was water, lots of it. She saw Rose but could not reach her. John was there laughing. Craig came in from another room. His hands were up in surrender, and someone who she did not recognize was behind him. A shot rang out, and blood was everywhere.

Susan woke up sweating and screaming. Someone was pounding on the front door, and she stumbled to it asking who it was. Craig announced it was him. She let him in and staggered back to the couch, depositing herself.

"Are you alright?"

The urgency in his voice snapped her awake.

"Yes. Why? What happened?"

"I overheard you screaming and thought you were being hurt." He tossed his briefcase on the nearby table and shut the door.

In a matter of seconds he stood over her. She could feel beads of perspiration swimming down her forehead. Craig left the room and returned with a damp washcloth, gently wiping her face.

The moisture from the cloth extinguished the fire burning her face. She was slightly aware of his body against hers as she leaned back, and he knelt into the couch. She closed her eyes, and for a change enjoyed the sensation of having someone nurse her.

The coolness swept over her blazing cheeks, down to the heat in her neck and making its way down to the warmth of her chest. Her eyes shot open, looking into Craig's soft expression. She started to protest, but he put his finger to her lips.

"You need to cool down. Don't resist me. I am not going to hurt you. You should know that by now."

Did she? Could she trust him? After the phone call, and the ledgers she had discovered in his office? What about the blue folder with information on Rose that he was in possession of?

He was right about needing to get her body heat down. Her core temperature had to be in the hundreds, and besides, she did not have the strength now to fight him off.

"I'm going in the kitchen to refresh the washcloth. Why don't you make yourself comfortable and lie down?" He exited the room.

She called out to him that she was fine.

"If you're sure, I'll just grab a glass of water and join you in the living room," he responded.

"Get me one as well, please." She was more interested in finding out why Craig came to her apartment, than him bathing her to cool down.

Chapter 11

Susan tossed on a forest green jogging suit, then came back into the living room. She noticed he took a seat on the chair across from the sofa. She took her position on the couch. As she lifted her glass to take a drink, he leaned forward to speak.

"I came upon something, and I need you to be completely honest with me."

"This sounds serious." She placed her water back on the coffee table.

"It is. I need to know about Rose." His stare was fixed on her eyes.

"Rose?" She gave him a quizzical expression.

"Yes. Rose Mullican."

"I am not aware of whom you're talking about." She lied, but she was not sure if she could trust him enough to tell him.

"Yes, you do. We talked about her before at the More for Your Money store." His jaw tightened up.

He was right. She would give him the same answer she did then.

"Oh yeah. She is a distant relative."

He shot up suddenly, startling her.

"Darn it, Susan! Don't play games with me. She's not a distant relative. I have knowledge of her missing, and she's someone close to you, and you need to tell me about her, now!" Craig glared down at her. He knew something and the only way she was going to find out was to be honest with him, to a degree.

"Okay, I'll tell you."

He sat back down, staying focused on Susan.

"But first will you promise to help me find her?"

She needed his assurance and see it in his eyes before she would open up to him.

"Yes, I vow to do whatever it takes."

"Rose is my younger sister."

"Why didn't you tell me about her before?"

Susan arose and walked nervously around to the back of the couch, feeling too uneasy to stay sat. He had questions, and some of them she could not answer. Not yet anyway. She had gone against what John and Detective Mike Holmes had told her not to do, which was give out any admission about Rose. Especially about being her sister.

John had briefed her about Craig having a blue folder containing information concerning Rose. She wanted the facts Craig had. To obtain her answers, she would be expected to supply some.

"A friend of mine, who is helping me locate her, told me it would be better if I didn't tell anyone. Including the law. He does, however, rely on an acquaintance from the police department working undercover."

"Is there any particular reason why he said not to let anyone know?"

"He said mentioning Rose's disappearance would appear bad for the company."

Craig rose to his feet and strode over to Susan.

"Let me get this straight," he began. "This friend of yours knows your sister is missing, and because of his business, he doesn't want to go public with this? That doesn't make sense to me. What would that have to do with Rose?"

"Craig, it's not as simple as that. It would involve me going to the beginning of her disappearance, and I am losing time. I need to find her. You said you are in possession of information about her."

Her eyes pleaded with him to tell her. He stepped over to the table where he had thrown his briefcase earlier. Opening it, he pulled out the blue folder.

"The blue folder," she gasped out. John was right about Craig having it.

"You recognize this?" He held out the folder, waving it a bit, with confusion written on his face.

"What?" She realized she spoke out loud. "My friend said there was a blue folder floating around somewhere that had something about Rose in it. Is that the same one?"

"I am not sure if it is, but it does include some insight about her. You talk a lot about your friend. Who is helping you?" The squinting in his eyes gave her the impression he knew.

Still, she debated on telling him. If John wanted Craig to be aware that she knew about the two of them, he would tell Craig. What she could not figure out was why John acted as if though he had no knowledge of Craig when she talked to him. He had some reason. Maybe to protect her. In the years she and John spent together, he had good intentions for his actions.

"I can't tell you."

"Why not?" His brow raised, challenging her.

She shifted from one foot to the other before speaking.

"He is not involved with Rose's disappearance, and I would rather keep him out of this."

"If he's helping you find Rose, isn't he already involved?" He held a smirk on his face.

"Yes, but he asked for his name to be kept out. He's gotten me this far, and he was right about the blue folder, so I'm going to hold to my promise."

"Okay, Miss Mullican. Let's sit down and go over this." He motioned toward the couch, and she readily obeyed.

The intent expression on his face as he was skimming through the pages caused some uneasiness in the pit of her stomach. He looked up from his reading before hesitating.

"Can you think of who would kidnap your sister?"

Kidnapped. There it was. The reason for Rose disappearing. She had to make sure.

"Does it say she was kidnapped?"

"It doesn't go into details, but the inkling is she's being held against her will somewhere. It does not say who is responsible, which I should have figured. And no exact location, just an area. Whoever is holding her is bad news. I cannot figure out who planted this in my office. Do you have an idea?"

"What do you mean by planted it? And how would I know?"

"I discovered the folder on my desk after you were snooping around in there. So, you had the access."

"You're telling me it wasn't in your possession all along?"

His eyebrows rose. "Oh, and who told you that? Your *friend?*" Sarcasm hit in his last words.

Susan was taken back. "Well, yes he did, but he had good resource for the information." She watched as his pearly white teeth slowly emerged through his tensed lips. His golden eyes glazed over.

"I'm getting tired of this buddy of yours. Whatever kind of assistance he is to you, he is misleading you miserably. If you do not want to tell me who he is, that is fine. Evidently this guy has no idea of what he is doing. Or he does, and you're headed for trouble." Midway through the last sentence the mocking tone was replaced with worry.

"Trust me, sugar. I'm not going to mislead you, and I'm not going to let anything bad happen to you." He paused for a moment, staring intently into her eyes.

"After reading a part in the folder, I have come to the decision it is too dangerous for you to stay here. The only way I can protect you is for you to come with me."

"What did you read that makes you believe I'm in danger? And what do you mean you have decided? I think I have the final say so." She scowled at him.

"Toward the end it mentioned plucking the pedals of the rose and the sweet smelling red one beside it. I can only assume you are the red one, since you do wear the sweet-smelling Red perfume." A sparkle crossed his eyes. "The person who wrote that story," he flicked at the pages with his right hand, "must be familiar with you and your sister."

She did not want to believe what he was saying, but inwardly she felt he might be right. Of all the people in her circle she could not understand why anyone would want to harm her or her sister.

The only theory she had to go on was Rose had found out about the drug dealing going on. Maybe the people who captured her thought Susan knew as well. And if so, would Craig be in on it?

Perhaps her best bet would be to find out where he was talking about going to. She could always go there herself.

"Come with you? Where?"

"In this folder it tells of a town south of here where Rose is being held in. I own a home not too far from there where we can stay while we search for her."

She pressed him further. "Which town, exactly?"

"So, are you saying you'll come with me?"

She stared blankly at him, not knowing how to answer that question. If she said no, he might not tell her. She could say yes, and not go, but she would be taking a chance he would either lie to her or follow her to the town.

Excitement about finding Rose hit, but so did the anxiety of going off alone with Craig. Was it a coincidence he had a place nearby? Aside from that, if what he said was true about Rose, how could she not go with him?

She made her way around to the back of the couch, running her fingers through the plush beige velvet material. She had to make a tough decision.

"How can I trust you?"

He moved from his seat and came up behind her. He placed his hands on her upper arms, and his lips maneuvered through her hair as his mouth edged closer to her ear.

"The only thing I can tell you is you can."

"What about what happened before at the other store?"

She turned to face him. Their bodies barely touching, their eyes locked together, and their lips were only inches away from each other.

"That situation before is irrelevant to the circumstances now. It's very crucial to find your sister, and I want to help you find her."

"Why is it important to you?"

"I care about people. Mainly those who are in danger like you and your sister are. Plus I have friends in the law enforcement down there who will aide us in finding Rose."

In a matter of seconds their lips were sealed together. She yielded to the kiss and wrapped her arms around his neck. He drew in her body, molding it into his.

His mouth teased her senses as it made its way to her ear, leaving trails of kisses behind. His soft-spoken voice carried a spark, lighting up her inside. "Please, Susan, come with me?"

Her conscience was demanding her to make a rational decision, while the kiss she invited cunningly played on her sub-conscious, swaying her to follow him. She was apprehensive about Craig, but the sincerity in his words was showing her she could trust him, to a point. Had she stepped over that point?

Chapter 12

Breathlessly Susan pulled away from Craig. She had to recompose her posture and escape from his embrace.

"Craig, you said you knew the police down there, but I was told not to involve them."

"You were evidently told many things, and some of them are not true. In this case you need to consider letting the law in on this."

"Why?"

"Because they can put away the *scums* responsible for kidnapping Rose. Besides, what had you planned on doing once you found her? Did you think these people were going to let you take off with her and not come after you?" He placed his hands on his hips.

His words stung Susan's intelligence.

"Well, I hadn't thought about that."

Craig nodded in agreement. "This is definitely why the police should be in on it. And what about this officer you mentioned earlier who is working undercover to find Rose? Did he have any leads?"

"Just to The Five and Dime."

"What did he say about it?"

"That her social security number showed up as her being employed there. You worked at that store for some time. Did you notice her?"

"No, I haven't. And her number has not crossed my desk. I review everyone when they come to work."

"I'd like to check out what you have about Rose. I want to make sure of my next move." Confidence in finding her sister had reclaimed its way back to Susan.

He snatched up the folder, took a page out of it placing it in her hands.

Rose had come up missing the same time the paper said, and the article described things that no one would have knowledge of, except the kidnapper. She was not familiar with the area it mentioned, but Craig said he was. Still, she had questions if he had something to do with Rose's disappearance. There was only one way to find out.

"Okay, I'll go."

"Great." He clasped his hands together. "We'll leave early in the morning. Be ready around two thirty with bags packed."

"Two thirty! That doesn't give me much time at all. I need to try to reach John." She bellowed it out before she had time to think. Craig's eyebrows dropped.

"John? Is this your friend you've been talking about?"

"Yes, but his name isn't important. I've got to call him and tell him what's going on."

"It isn't John Lancett, is it?" Disgust hit in his words.

"I told you it doesn't matter. I'll be ready in the morning. I'll plan on you being here then."

She darted off to the front door to open it for him to leave, but as she rounded him, Craig reached out, grabbed her arm, and turned her to face him. Amusement danced in his eyes, spilling over to his lips.

"On second thought, I think we'll change plans a little. Go ahead and put some of your things together, and we will go to my place for the night, leaving out from there in the morning." His eyebrows rose, synchronized with the corners of his mouth.

"I think I'll feel more comfortable with the other plan where you pick me up here at two thirty." She had blurted out about John, and now she was apprehensive of what to expect from Craig.

His expression softened as he spoke.

"Look, sugar, nothing bad is going to happen to you from me. I don't want you to let anyone know where we're going, because this is very dangerous. The less trouble we can invite, the better off we are."

"If I don't tell him, he's going to worry. He's been helping me find Rose, and he's concerned about what happened to her." She hesitated for a moment. "John has been part of our family for at least ten years. I think I owe him the decency of informing him of what's happening." She searched out his eyes, seeing what reaction he would have to the details she just gave out.

He narrowed his eyes. "Are you *really* familiar with Lancett? I mean as in his dealings?"

"I-I would hope so. He's been sort of distant lately, but I assumed that's because of his new responsibilities."

Craig raked his fingers through his soft brown hair and pursed his lips. He was keeping something from Susan about John, but she was not sure what it could be.

"Why don't we just for now not concern ourselves about Lancett, and you pack so we can be on our way?"

Still uncertain about this change of plans, she nevertheless agreed.

Once in her bedroom, she dragged out her American Tourist luggage. Running her fingers over the decal, she remembered the day she had bought it. It had been a day of freedom. She was moving to Louisiana to go to college, and away from her controlling parents and bratty little sister.

Her parents had wanted her to take over the corporation one day that they had struggled early on to build, but she had had other goals in mind. Rose had followed after them by taking classes in high school on business.

She longed for those days back, instead of going off with a man she hardly knew anything about.

What did she know about Craig Summers? Or was it Bryers, the name he had given at the More for Your Money store? She knew he was hiding something. Undoubtedly it had something to do with the drug sales going on in the stores the newspaper wrote about. That knowledge unsettled her even more about going off with him. But to find her sister, she would go.

"Are you about ready?" Craig peeked around the corner, and then puckered his lips glancing into her empty suitcase.

"You're going to be tired of wearing the same outfit after a while." Specks of gold in his eyes glistened off the bedroom light.

"I'm sorry. It's hard for me to pack for somewhere I have never been to before. What is the weather like down there?"

She watched him enter her room. His movements were slick like a panther. He kept eye contact as he came closer to her, causing her heart to flutter. The air about him was mystical, and her weakness for more of his caresses was trying to take over as he stopped inches from her.

His voice held a hint of passion. "South Texas is warm around this time. In the mornings, the cool mist blows in from the bay. I would recommend a light jacket and shorts. Now, do you need help packing?" He raised his brows.

If he lingered any longer the desire for him building up inside would take over. She had to push those feelings aside and hustle him out of the room. Her reaction to him put her off guard. She had to ensure of his motives and intentions toward her before she was duped to more of his kisses.

"No, thank you. I can handle it from here." Her lips quivered as they formed a smile. He brushed his thumb across the corner of her mouth, sparking yet another flame inside, exploring her eyes with his.

"Okay, but don't be long. We need to leave shortly."

He strolled out of the room pausing long enough at the doorway to wink at her, then disappeared.

She threw some summer dresses, shorts, and tops along with a wind breaker, shawl, and sandals in her suitcases. In the bathroom she tossed in her toiletries. The only other item she packed was the unicorn carousel she bought at the auction house for Rose.

With everything ready to go they headed toward Craig's car. Mrs. Robertson and Lady came up to them as they were loading it.

"Oh, Susan, are you going somewhere?" She gestured at the luggage she and Craig were positioning in the trunk.

Susan glanced over at him, and his eyes were stern.

"Yes, but only for a short time."

"I see." The older woman shifted her gaze to him, giving him a once over, then back to her. "Are you and your male friend going on a vacation together?"

"My sister needs my help, so Craig was nice enough to offer to take me." She did not lie about the situation. Just altered it a bit.

"Is she sick?"

Mrs. Robertson kept pushing questions at her, and she tried to hurry up before she said too much.

"You could say that."

"Is there anything I can do?"

Susan handed Craig her toiletry bag, and he placed it into the trunk of his black BMW along with the rest of her luggage.

"No but thank you anyway."

He stood beside Susan. "We need to go if we're going to beat the five o'clock traffic."

"My, you two looks like such a cute couple." The older woman was starry eyed. "How long will you be gone?"

"I am not sure. Hopefully not long."

"I'll keep an eye on your place while you're gone."

"Thank you." Susan could not fight off the compulsion to give her a hug. She had not known her long, but she was a sweet woman. Almost like an aunt. She bent down and petted Lady on the head and told her to take care of her companion. In return, the pooch licked her on the face several times.

"You're an adorable dog," Susan said.

Lady pranced over to Craig, and jumped up on his leg, wagging her tail. He laughed and brushed her fur.

She glanced over at Mrs. Robertson and thought she saw tears in her eyes. "Are you going to be alright?"

"My goodness, yes child. I hate seeing you go, but I understand when your family needs you. I'll see you when you get back. You look after her, young man."

"Yes, ma'am. I promise."

Craig smiled at Susan. He seemed sincere, but she could not help questioning about her trip with him. Was she headed for a set-up?

Chapter 13

The silence in the car as Craig drove to his house caused Susan to ponder what he was thinking. They hit the edge of town, and in front of them laid a vast amount of wilderness. Enough forested area for someone to vanish in without anyone knowing. The thought made her nervous, forming a knot in her stomach.

"Are we getting close to your place?" She tried suppressing the anxiety building up inside her throat.

He swiftly glanced her up and down, then turned his attention back to the road. His features softened as he spoke.

"It's another five minutes away. There is no reason for you to be afraid. I told you I would not harm you, and I meant what I said."

He gave Susan a re-assuring smile.

His words calmed her some, but she was still uneasy about what to expect being alone with him.

She could not bring herself to believe he would do bodily injury to her. Emotionally he could. He had shown her by the tender kiss he gave her back at her apartment that he desired her. A desire she had a hard time resisting.

A couple of more minutes passed before they pulled up to a one-story house. Craig brought her overnight bag and toiletry case inside with them.

Going through the house she noticed the living room was fashionably lavished with black leather and dark mahogany wood. They continued down a hallway stopping long enough for him to switch on the hall light. Out of curiosity she tried to glimpse into the opened rooms as they passed by. The glare from the overhead did not offer much sight into them, but she detected a desk in one. The other one looked more like a storage room.

Craig passed through the third doorway, and a glow emerged. She followed him and found herself in a medium-sized bedroom. Inside were a dresser and an antique bed covered with a quilt that had the appearance of being around for a while. An old-fashioned alarm clock stood on a little table sitting by the bed.

"This is my grandparents' house, and this was my grandmother's room. I hope you don't mind sleeping in here tonight."

"It is a nice room. You said this used to be your grandmother's room? She didn't die in here, did she?"

"No, she died in a nursing home not too far from here, as did my grandfather. Why do you ask?"

Susan hesitated a bit. "Well, my grandmother died in her sleep in her bedroom. I was only five at the time, but I still remember the odor of stench, and the sense of gloom."

Craig gently swiped the stray hair out of Susan's face, and caressed her shoulder.

"We'll be heading off as planned at two thirty. If you want to shower, the bathroom is the next door down. I'll put us a little something together to keep the hunger pains down." Craig ambled out of the room.

Susan hauled up her luggage and carefully placed it on the bed, searching inside until she uncovered her nightshirt and shorts. She took them and her toiletry bag in her arms.

Going out the doorway she glanced down the hall, and a closed door caught her attention. Craig was busy in the kitchen, giving her time to venture down toward the room. She opened the door, and from the light of the hallway, there appeared to be a crib inside. Was he married and had a child? If so, where was his wife and baby?

"The bathroom is in the other direction." Irritation laced in Craig's voice behind her and observed his hand as he almost slammed the door shut in front of her face. She was afraid to turn and face him, because she knew she stepped over the line, and he had every reason to be upset with her.

"I'm sorry, Craig." She shifted around, clutching her belongings to her bosom. "I had no right to open that door." She moved her eyes up to meet his. He glared down at her, but his eyes held pain in them instead of anger.

"No, you didn't. I would suggest you stay clear of this room. Dinner will be ready shortly." He shot back into the kitchen.

She hastily proceeded to the bathroom and closed the door with her heart beating fast. She was never one for confrontation, especially when she was at fault.

After her shower, the decision whether to go into the room she resided in and stay there for the evening or meet him in the dining room when the meal was ready faced her. The aroma from his cooking had seeped up her nostrils, luring her stomach to go peek at the dinner.

After depositing her things into the bedroom, she approached the kitchen. Craig stood over the stove with a plate in his hand. She took the few seconds she had and leaned against the door jamb to eye him while his back was to her.

His shoulders reminded her of a quarterback, strong and massive. The unyielding t-back shirt displayed a lean, but very muscular body. There was little fat on his arms, if any, and his biceps told on him that he worked out. His hips, in perfect line with his torso, teasingly presented a tight butt. The bare legs under the sport shorts were those of an athlete who ran marathons for a living.

He pivoted in her direction, and she immediately adjusted her eyes to his face.

"Like what you see?" He lifted his eyebrows at her. Her cheeks became fiery hot and decided to change the subject.

"I was seeing if dinner is ready. I'm a little famished." She gave out a curt smile, trying to hide her embarrassment.

His eyes scanned her down and back up. When their eyes met, pleasure was written on his, apparently enchanted with her attire.

"You've arrived just in time. I have a plate of burritos prepared for you. Also, I took the liberty of pouring you a glass of milk. Go ahead and take this into the dining room. I'll join you in a minute." He handed her a dish and turned his attention back to the stove as she proceeded into the adjoining room.

On the table, which seated six, were two glasses across from each other, along with a fork and knife on a napkin.

She usually drank milk with her meals, but she did not like the fact that he decided what she should drink. The more she was around Craig, the more she realized how dominating he was.

She sat on the other side and surveyed him as he came in with his plate and settled down.

"Did you try it yet?" His boyish grin was fishing for a compliment.

"No, I decided to wait on you, and see if you eat it first." She chided him.

She looked on as he dug into his burrito, cutting it with a knife. The aroma enticed her stomach even more, and she delved into hers whole-heartedly. The tenderness of the vegetables and meat plus the tantalizing taste of the seasonings melted with savoring flavor. It was to die for.

"You must either like it, or you're starving to death."

Her fork stopped midway in route to her mouth, and she glanced up, noticing Craig smiling at her. "Why do you say that?"

"Because I don't recall seeing anyone enjoying a burrito like that."

"Well, both. It is good, and I have not eaten all day, unless you count a protein drink from this morning. So, I'm starving as well." She continued with her forks journey.

After swallowing the last fork full of food and chasing it down with the milk, she confronted him with her needs.

"Craig, it is imperative I get hold of someone to take care of my things back at my apartment, and my car."

He shrugged his shoulders. "I've already done that," then finished off his meal.

"You did? When?"

"While you were in the shower." He presented a satisfied smile.

"I don't like people I'm not familiar with messing in my business."

"If I didn't, who would you've appointed? Lancett?"

He threw John's last name out of his mouth like a lion spewing out a piece of bad meat. She wanted to ask him how he knew John, but if she did, he would probably want the history of her and him. Now was not the time. Uncertainty still loomed over where she stood between them. John had rubbed Craig the wrong way for some reason.

"I didn't say I was going to get him to do it."

"You don't have to. Some things I have perceptions about."

"Oh, and how?" Susan dared him.

"Because I'm-" he hesitated for a moment. "I know. Let's leave it at that."

She could tell he was going to give something up about himself, but what? That he was a crook, and could tell when someone was lying to him?

Chapter 14

"Craig," Susan did not ask him her question before she was interrupted.

Who could be calling now? Craig thought as his cellphone rang. Getting up from the table, he excused himself into the kitchen.

"Craig, this is Roy. Officer Humphrey. I hope I caught you before you left town."

"You did. Why? What's going on?" He walked toward the living room, putting enough distance between him and Susan, not wanting her to overhear his conversation.

"We found the guy who held you and your lady friend up. Unfortunately, seems someone else got to him first. He was behind a dumpster. Dead."

"You're sure he is the same person?"

"Yes. His prints matched the ones on the gun at the scene involving you."

"Were you able to make an identification on him?"

"Web Lewis. He had several run-ins with the police. He was also linked to the Cartel gang." Craig could hear the satisfaction in Roy's voice. He continued on. "We received an inside tip that the Cartel instructed him to hold you up."

"Why would they do that?"

"They think you are an undercover cop and were searching for your badge. The lieutenant said to inform you he's sending Tony Kelley and Randall Maxwell with you to Port Emerald."

"Why in blazes is he doing that? I do not need any FBI people watching over me. I'm quite capable of taking care of myself", he said, struggling to keep his voice down.

Craig had nothing personal against the two men. He had enjoyed their company on other occasions when deemed necessary for them to be present. Not this time. There was no need to be babysat.

"For one, they handle kidnap cases when drugs are involved. Two, he believes you are being led away from the original case. He wants more insight about your lady friend. Is she someone you can trust?"

Craig became infuriated. Not only was he told about having two uninvited guests, now the decision he made was being questioned by his own Lt. Dan Johnson.

"Look, you carry the word back that I did my investigation on my *lady friend,* and I'm quite happy with my finding. Kelley and Maxwell are fine. Tell them I'll meet them at Quick Stop at the edge of town when I make it in." Craig clicked the end button on the phone as soon as he strained the last words out.

He was a little harder on Humphrey than he should have been. Roy was only following orders. Ones he did not agree with. He had not intended to take his frustration out on him.

The gunman was one problem he did not need to concern himself about. His death was unfortunate, but probably better than if he had gotten hold of him.

He made his way back into the dining room to retrieve the dinner dishes.

* * *

"The burritos were delicious. Thank you. For that meal, I'll do the washing." She pushed her plate aside.

"That sounds like some good news." The tone he used told Susan the call he just received was anything but, perking her curiosity up.

"Is everything okay?"

Craig took his attention from gathering the dishes to her. "The officer at the scene the other day at the auction house just called. He said they found the man who held us up, but he was dead."

"Did they identify who he was?"

"Web Lewis. Some unknowns nobody trying to make a buck illegally."

"Web Lewis? The name sounds familiar from somewhere." She concentrated until a face came up. "Of course! He was at my father's corporation." She did not realize she said it out loud, until the sound of Craig dropping the silverware on to the plates, and a very audible 'what' coming out of his mouth. Focused on his face, she anticipated on some explaining to do.

"Oh boy."

"Oh boy is right, Ms. Mullican. Tell me what is going on."

"Can we go somewhere where there are no knives?"

"Why? So you don't put another one in my back?"

"Now that was uncalled-for. I am aware there are some things I've not told you, but if you're honest with me, you haven't been entirely up front with me either."

He held up his hands. "You're right, you're right. Tell you what. While you do the dishes, I will make us some coffee, and we can sit in the living room and talk. Does that sound fair?"

"Yes." They scooped up the dinnerware and headed towards the kitchen.

Susan contemplated on how much she should tell him about John, and her role concerning him. Should she have to give up something, he would too. They were in cahoots together on something, and she wanted to know what.

Craig handed her a towel to dry her hands off with when she finished. When she gave it back to him, he exchanged it with a cup, and motioned his hand to the other room.

He sat on the black leather love seat, and she lowered herself on to the matching chair. He placed a coaster near her, and he put his mug on one.

There was silence for a few moments before Craig broke it.

"Well, I'm waiting." He was intent.

"I thought you were going to start this talk off."

He leaned forward, searching her eyes closely. "Alright, I'll go first. Who is Web Lewis?"

"I am not too familiar with him. All I know is he was employed at my father's corporation."

"You mentioned it earlier, but why would he want to harm you, or me?"

"That I can't answer." She took a sip of her coffee. It was still hot, and burned her mouth, bringing tears to her eyes. She moved the cup away from her without spilling any fluid. Craig got up and came back with a glass of ice, tipping it toward her.

"Here, suck on one of these. They help relieve the pain."

"You must have done this before," she said as she took the glass from him.

"Oh yeah." He sat back down in his spot. "Back to our questions. Why didn't you recognize Lewis if he worked for your father?"

"If you remember right, he grabbed me from behind. I could not make out anything about him except his brown shoulder-length hair. Nor did I catch much of his face besides his profile. The only other thing I caught about him was his sweat suit and the smell."

"Let me ask another question. How are you acquainted with John Lancett?"

She hesitated before answering. "He also works for my father's corporation. How do you know him?"

"He's someone who came to me wanting me to give you a job. I did not realize why, until now. What I don't understand is how Rose's disappearance has anything to do with the case I am working on."

The last sentence sounded strange to her. "What do you mean by a case you are working on? Are you a cop?"

He stood and paced the floor a few times before returning to his seat.

Susan kept her eyes on him and patiently waited for him to come clean with her. She peered deeply into his golden eyes as he spoke.

"I'm an undercover drug enforcement agent." He paused for a moment then continued. "The two stores you and I had worked at were under surveillance for narcotic activities. Shortly after you left the first store, it was shut down."

"What about the Five and Dime?" She should be perplexed by what he had just told her about him being a DEA, but she took it in stride. Especially since she was right about drugs being run in the stores.

* * *

"Arrangements are being made to close it down as well. Why the concern?"

"I had a hunch about the drugs. Although, I figured you to be the ringleader, considering you were at both facilities. You are who you say you are, aren't you?" She raised a questioning brow.

He let out a small chuckle, and then reached for his badge in his back pocket, displaying it to her. After she took a real close look, she leaned back into the chair with satisfaction written on her face.

"So, now we are straight on whom I am, we can continue on with finding your sister. Do you think Lancett might be involved with your sister's kidnapping?"

"I should hope not! He is the one who's been helping me find her. If not for him and Mike Holmes, I would not be this far. Are you sure you did not kidnap her? After all, you are the one holding the folder containing information about her."

"As I told you before, it was planted in my office. Who is this Mike Holmes you just mentioned?"

"He is the policeman working on finding Rose. Which is a good reason for me to contact John, so they don't put out a missing person's report on me." She glared at him, then proceeded to stand. He held out a hand grabbing hers, sitting her back down.

"You don't need to. I've already taken care of Lancett."

"Boy, you just take care of everything, don't you? It would be better if I talk to him. He's expecting me to call in every so often."

"Just let it go for tonight. It is getting late, and we will be waking up early so we can arrive at Port Emerald before it gets dark. There's not much time to waste."

He had more questions to ask her, but she was trying his patience with her compulsion about calling Lancett. And the nagging pain in the back of his neck reared its ugly head. He tried to rub it out but only a hot shower would do it this time.

"That's fine, Craig. I can always call him tomorrow."

She finished off her drink and huffed off into the kitchen with her cup. He heard her washing the dish, and then take off towards her room. He sat there for a few minutes, sipping on his coffee.

The shower eased the tension headache, until he lied down, and his mind went into overdrive. He was relieved when the lieutenant gave him the go ahead to jump from the previous assignment of money laundering and drug dealing to finding Susan's sister. It helped his argument by telling him Rose's disappearance tied into the original case. Craig knew it did somehow but unsure in what way.

It had to do with the people involved. Susan and Rose Mullican, John Lancett, Web Lewis, and now Mike Holmes.

Holmes had surprised him. Even though they worked in different departments at the precinct, their friendship, he had thought, was tight. He did not share all his cases with Craig, but he had known Craig was working undercover at the More for Your Money Store. Which makes him question why Mike had not told him about Rose coming up missing.

The other four were connected through Susan. Lancett was his inside man to the laundering of drugs. Web was the scum who had held him and Susan up by gunpoint. But he could not fit the two women into the scheme the Cartel had going on.

He trusted they stood on the innocent end. Maybe Rose found out something adequate to put the head honcho away. Jeremy DeVore had persuaded his little brother, Kenny, to get involved in drugs. Even more reason to find her, for the information needed to convict the *slime*.

Susan, he discovered, was searching for her sister, but she was not telling him everything about Lancett. She said he was a friend, but if she knew he had a part in the drug running, why wouldn't she turn him in? Did her father's company have something to do with the Cartel? What was the company's business?

She was very persistent about letting Lancett know of her where-abouts, and where she was at was in his house. A house that had not held a woman for a long time, or anyone else.

He had kept that door closed to the room containing the crib ever since the so-called accident. He did not have the time or gumption to clean it out. Or maybe, as hard as it was to admit, he had not gotten over the fact Lillian and their unborn son were gone...forever.

Chapter 15

Craig turned over, shutting the screaming alarm off. It was one-thirty in the morning. He just barely got to sleep.

Making his way to the bathroom, he splashed water on his face to help wake-up. He did not detect any movement in the house to alert him if Susan was stirring yet, so he walked down to the room she occupied.

The light was off, but he made out a figure in the bed. He knew she must have been tired but did not change the fact he had to rouse up sleeping beauty. He hesitated for a moment before switching on the overhead. The image turned out to be her overnight case.

The search for her ended when his nose caught the tantalizing aroma of maple. Upon entering the kitchen, he relished the scene ahead of him.

He took in the backside of this mysterious woman cooking bacon and tossing eggs around like a pro. Vaguely he recognized her humming as a song being popular with the youth. It had played on Joey's radio at work. Her hips swayed to the rhythm. Every once in a while, her auburn hair would brush her shoulders as she flipped her head from side to side.

He could easily play into her movements. Come up behind her, wrapping her up in his embrace, and snuggle into her neck breathing in the sweet scent of Red she wore.

It could lead into a more provocative dance; one he did not want to act on. Especially now. He was trying to keep their relationship simple this time. At the first store it had been built on lies.

Now they are mindful about the other, or at least what they told each other. There were still things she was hiding from him; he was sure of. She had not told him the truth about Lancett, a man who Craig despised.

And he had a few things he kept from Susan. One was the FBI people coming to Summersville. She had enough problems without having to worry about being under surveillance.

He cleared his throat, startling her. She turned her head in his direction, and the surprised look was replaced by a pleasant smile. Her hazel eyes sparkled under the light.

"I hope you don't mind if I made breakfast this morning. I had a hard time sleeping and woke up before the alarm went off. We do have time before we leave, don't we?"

"Since you are almost done with the cooking part, I don't see why not. The aroma of the bacon alone swayed my stomach."

* * *

They walked their plates over to the little kitchen table. Outside the darkness of the world flooded through the bay windows. A darkness Susan herself felt since Rose had disappeared.

She observed Craig digging into his eggs, being careful when he dipped his toast into the running yolks. She tried a couple of bites, but her hunger faded away.

"This is excellent. Why aren't you eating?"

"Thinking about Rose, how she's doing, and if she's still alive."

Craig put his fork down, giving full attention to Susan. "I believe she is."

"Why do you think so?"

"Look at it this way, if she were dead, whoever planted that information in my office wouldn't go to all the trouble. Evidently someone wants her found for some reason. And if that someone was your friend, Lancett, he has some explaining to do."

"Why would you think it was him?"

"He told you about me having the folder, am I right?" She nodded in response. "His car was also seen at the store around the same day that popped up. Now I am unaware of what your relationship is with Lancett, and it is none of my business. He is part of the drug Cartel, and I would like to know what his position is at your father's corporation. It could link to some of this mystery of your sister's disappearance." He clasped his hands together, leaning on them underneath his chin, while steadily gazing into Susan's eyes.

"John is a trusted friend who worked for my father for over ten years. I have a hard time believing he caters to anything to do with some drug Cartel, or with Rose's disappearance."

"If you don't believe he does, then what would it hurt telling me what office he holds?"

"Fine, he's the president of the corporation." She flung her words at him.

"That's strange. Wouldn't your father be?"

"He would, if he were alive." She quivered a little. It still distressed her to think of him, and her mother gone.

"I'm sorry. I did not know. We need to leave soon if we are going to make Summersville while it is still daylight. I will get the dishes. Do you have everything ready?"

She brought her bags into the living room and sat down in the chair waiting for him. He emerged from the hallway with a few of his own.

"Let's go," was all he said as they headed out the front door, into the car, and down the road.

* * *

During the trip she had had more time to mull over in her mind the past week. She was surprised Craig was an undercover drug enforcement agent, and extremely glad he was on the side of the law.

The night before he said John had come to him wanting him to hire her at the store. More than likely to help her find Rose.

Earlier before they left, he insisted John was involved with the drug

Cartel. She could not see that happening. Craig had to be mistaken. John was not that kind of person.

They made small talk along the way, but both avoided any heavy conversation. Even when they stopped to eat, pumped gas, or stretch their legs.

The scenery changed from an abundance of pine trees and oaks to open space spotted with palm trees and scrub brushes. The familiar fragrance of piney woods turned to a salty, fishy scent that left a bad taste in Susan's mouth and weighed heavy on her face.

Upon entering the tiny town of Port Emerald, they pulled up to a convenient store where a scarce amount of people was coming in and out. Craig asked if she wanted anything to drink. She said yes and her preference of soda.

She eyed Craig walking up to two men dressed in suits standing outside a blue Sedan and shook their hands. One was tall and lanky with brown hair. The other man was a little shorter, with a dark complexion, and brown wavy hair turning gray, along with his neatly trimmed beard and mustache.

* * *

"Maxwell, that key I just slipped you goes to my uncle's house. The directions are folded up in the paper. Find some place to hang out at until ten. I don't want Ms. Mullican knowing what's going on."

Tony, the younger of the two, spoke up.

"She doesn't know about us?"

"Haven't you learned anything in these past couple of years, mate?" Randall chided Tony. "You don't go telling people what to expect. Particularly when they're the prime suspect."

Those words ignited Craig's temper.

"She's not a prime suspect. I have my reasons for not disclosing to her everything. For now, she knows I am an undercover DEA, and I am helping her find her sister. I'll tell her about you two later." On a friendlier note he added they might want to buy some food for the house.

* * *

The two men glanced in her direction. They waved their good-byes. Craig proceeded into the store and came back out shortly with two sodas in his hand.

"So, were those friends of yours," Susan shot at him when he entered the car.

"What?"

"Those two guys you talked to before you went inside. Are they your friends?"

"Oh, yeah. Old acquaintances." He then changed the subject.

"We'll be going on the cause-way that goes over the Emerald Bay. To the right of it is Lighthouse Beach and RV Park with a mile-long pier. Lots of people go fishing at night on it which is well-lit with lights."

Craig reminded her of a scenic tour guide with the description he gave. His enthusiasm for the town showed.

They turned a bend in the road, and there laid the bridge and scenery just as he had mentioned. From a distance she saw a few people dotted along the pier.

A variety of recreational vehicles were situated at the park. She spotted one with a group of professionally dressed men standing around a map. She could not make out much more of the picture. The men quickly came out of her view as they headed up the bridge.

Craig turned down a small farm road, and she caught sight of a sign stating they were entering Summersville with the population of seventy-six. Two double story houses were in the distance. When they neared the residences, she noticed they stood on stilts. They pulled up under the second one.

"We're here," Craig said with a smile on his face.

"Where's here?"

"My aunt's house." He got out and began to unload the car.

When Susan got out, she drew in a deep breath. The odor gagged her.

"Why does it stink like fish around here?"

He chuckled at her with amusement in his eyes. "Follow me up the stairs and I'll show you."

The red steps leading up to the landing reminded her of a carpet laid out to welcome its visitors. The deck hugged the small cottage-like house on three sides.

Craig directed her attention to the east. It was a breathtaking view of quaint old houses mixed with the modern buildings. The sun gave the bay the appearance of a shimmering lake of quicksilver.

"This is why you smell fish. Invigorating, isn't it?"

"Maybe to you, but I have other words to define it."

"You'll get used to it after a day or two."

Craig was sure of himself. She had her doubts.

In a tree behind Susan some Mockingbirds sang to each other, and an owl hooted in the distance. The wind blew gently through her hair, whirling the ends around to her face. In the brushes below them she saw something moving, but she could not make it out until it emerged into a clearing.

"A rat! There are rats here?"

Craig laughed out loud. "That's a field mouse."

"I don't care what you call it, it's a rat."

Susan witnessed in astonishment as a rattlesnake quietly stalked the mouse and bit it. The process of the snake devouring its meal perplexed her.

A piercing gunshot sounded, and something whizzed past her, startling her. The snake jumped into the air with a puff of smoke coming from its head. As she turned, she observed Craig holding a gun.

Chapter 16

"Wh-what are you doing with a gun?" Susan's heart fluttered. She did not like those things.

"Need protection, don't we?" Craig gave a sheepish grin as he tucked the weapon behind his back.

"I thought you said we would be safe out here?"

"Sure, but you never know. Don't tell me you're afraid of guns?"

"No, I'm not. They are dangerous. When I was a little girl, I saw a friend of my mom's get killed by one." She felt a tear starting to swell in her eyes as she remembered that horrible night.

Craig softly brushed a strand of hair from her face. The tenderness of his hand, the faint scent of Stetson lingering around him, and the warmth in his eyes made her long for more of his touches. He gently lifted her chin up to his. He parted his lips, but instead of bending down to kiss her and keep her in the cloud she was in, he made a statement that brought her back to reality.

"It's the people who make them dangerous."

Inwardly she knew he was right, but she did not want to face that fact.

"So, this is your aunt's house?"

"Yep. My uncle built this one and the one next door back in the eighties. This one here they kept for me when I would come down to visit them."

"Where's your aunt?" Susan looked around. "Is she expecting us?"

A bit of sadness hit into Craig's eyes. "She passed away a few years ago."

"Oh, I'm sorry."

Craig moved to the front door unlocking it. "Don't be. She lived her life the way she wanted." Placing his hands on his hips, he narrowed his eyes. "Now, are you going to help me unload the car or are you expecting to be waited on?"

She helped with the luggage inside the small house. Susan took a minute looking around. Off to the left laid an open kitchen with a stove and refrigerator on one side. Across from the appliances a sink and some cabinets stood. A window centered the back wall, giving a peek out to the bay Craig had shown her.

To the right of her a round table with four chairs and two huge windows, one in the front and the other on the side, resided. The panes allowed the rays from the setting sun to bathe the dining area, stretching over toward the section of the house where a couch sat. The living room was smaller than the one she had at the apartment, but it had a cozy feeling. On top of the television she took notice of a wooden plaque with the name Summers engraved on it.

As Craig emerged out of the hallway, Susan quizzed him. "So, Summers is your real last name. Or is it a prop?"

He brought his brows together, and she pointed to the nameplate.

"Oh, yeah."

"I noticed the sign coming in said Summersville. Is this town named after you?"

"After my great grandfather, Steven Summers."

"The one who died in the nursing home?"

"No, that was my grandfather, one of Steven's sons. He moved away because of family altercations. Most of the Summers remained in this area, until the hurricane in the early sixties destroyed it as well as the original causeway bridge. The pier you saw along the new causeway is the remainder of the old. Shortly afterwards they rebuilt the town and named it Summersville after Steven."

He rubbed the back of his neck, something she had seen him doing when he was stressed out.

"Look, it's getting late so let's get settled in. Your things are in the middle room. There is no food here, so we will have to go to the store tomorrow. I packed a can of coffee and a couple of breakfast bars. It'll hold us over until then."

He stood for a moment, and Susan waited to see if he had anything else to say. She could tell he was tired, and so was she. The mentioning of going to bed sounded good to her. She would question him in the morning about where they could start looking for her sister at.

"Okay. Goodnight." She started toward the hall when Craig put his hand out. She stopped in her tracks and met his gaze.

"We didn't talk much about a plan on finding Rose at my grandparent's house, or on the drive down here. That is my fault. I am used to working by myself, and keeping things floating around in my head about what I am going to do. I will try to keep you informed on my plans. I do not know what to expect from this search. All hopes and prayers are we find her and that she's safe."

"I hope so too. This is the first real lead I've had to her, besides at The Five and Dime Store where Detective Mike Holmes said she would be."

He nodded in response. "Yes, and I'm beginning to believe we've been set up for something."

"More like I'm the one being set up, and for a fool. You are just someone who is caught amidst of it by helping me. But I don't understand why John and Mike would do this?"

"I hate to break this to you, sugar, but I'm not an innocent by-stander. Lancett told me to watch out for you whatever it took. He didn't tell me anything about Rose missing."

"So, you're only here because of John, not because you wanted to be?" She was crushed. She believed him back at her apartment when he said he was helping her because he cared about what happened to her and Rose.

"I want to help you more now than before and find out what's going on. I don't like being deceived."

"No, I don't guess you like being hoodwinked. But I am sorry to remind you, Mr. Summers, this is not about you and your pride. This is about finding my sister who is out there *somewhere* being held against her will. And if your only concern is yourself, then I don't need your help!"

Susan stormed off down the hallway leaving Craig standing with his mouth gaping.

* * *

Now what did I say? He tried to figure out what set her off. Did she think he did not care about her? Because if she thought he did not, she was far from being right. He did and more than what he should. Plus he was very much concerned about finding Rose.

Susan was correct when she had asked why Mike Holmes and Lancett had told her Rose worked at the last store. He could not understand why they were doing business together. Lancett's got more irons in this fire than he first thought. That made Lancett even more dangerous.

Lancett had contact with Boyd, the owner of the Five and Dime. It would not be long, and the feds would have the second logbook on the place showing the drug dealing going on.

Craig hated to think about what Boyd would do once he caught wind that he turned it in. There could be more trouble than he could handle. Craig was going to have to keep Susan safe and out of sight. Mostly out of touch with Lancett.

He had his suspicions about Lancett planting the blue notebook in his office. He would not be surprised if Lancett kidnapped Rose since he knew the family well. What would be his purpose? In the morning he would ask Susan what her father's corporation dealt in. There had to be a link between the company and the cartel.

* * *

A restless night, Craig thought as he forced himself out of bed and headed toward the kitchen. After making a pot of coffee, he looked out the window to the bay watching the sun come up over it. He missed seeing it in the time he had been away from there.

He walked over to the other side of the small cottage to see if his guests arrived at the other house. The blue Sedan sat near the stairs. Tony leaned on the balcony railing looking out toward the bay with a cup in his hand. His eyes latched on to Craig's and waved his hand. Craig returned it with one of his own and set out to the bathroom for a shower and shave.

While shaving his face, he heard a scream, and rushed to Susan's room where an overwhelming sight beheld him.

Chapter 17

Susan, in a frenzy, pulled her pants off.

"What's going on?" Concern laced Craig's voice.

"Something bit me!"

"Where?" His eyes darted around Susan's body looking for a possible insect bite. No one had lived at the house for some time, and no telling what attacked her.

"In my pants. I didn't see anything come out of them."

"Give them here."

She handed them to him following him into the living room. He took the slacks and shook them furiously. Something massive dropped out of them, and he crushed it with a nearby object and threw it in the trash can in the kitchen.

Susan stayed on his heels. "What was it? Am I going to die?"

He spun around and for the first time took in the soft pink shirt which barely covered the matching panties she wore. He decided to divert his attention.

"It was a scorpion."

"A scorpion!"

Craig nodded to her question, then took off to finish shaving his face. He knew if he stayed in the same room with her dressed like that, they would both find themselves in a position they did not want to be in at this time.

"Hold on, guy," Susan said as she reached for him. She had grabbed on to his biceps, which were normally rock hard. Under her grasp they were yielding. "What color was this scorpion?"

Frustrated he faced her. "I don't know. Brown, red, maybe black."

"What do you mean? Didn't you just kill it? You have to remember. My life depends upon it!"

The urgency in her voice stopped him to think. "Brown," he said with a sigh. "Now can I go back to what I was doing?"

He put his hands on his hips, and she took an extensive view of him. His shaving cream remained on half of his face, and moisture lingered on his body from the shower. He studied her face with amusement as her eyes trailed some drops of water running down his chest, resting on the red towel he had draped around his waist. She quickly raised her eyes back up to his. Embarrassment overshadowed her face, and it served her right.

"Yeah." Her words stumbled out. "I just need to put an ice pack on the back of my leg and stay off it for a while."

"Should be some trays in the freezer. Do you need any help?" The offer was innocent but teasing.

"No, I'll be fine." She hopped to the refrigerator, and Craig watched as she bounced off. He grumbled to himself as he went back into the bathroom to finish up preparing for the day.

He overheard her wrestling with the ice trays and jumping to the couch. While putting on a pair of pants, he decided to help her whether she wanted him to or not.

She sat up getting aggravated with trying to keep the flimsy bag of ice in place.

Shaking his head, he walked over to her and took the bag from her hand. She glared up at him as he told her to lie on her stomach. With resentment, she did.

The sting had caused a sizable welt on the backside of her thigh near her panties. In the process of placing the bag on the wound, his fingers brushed her undergarment.

"Hey!" Susan swung her head around to try to face him. "Watch where your hands go."

"That was an accident. The area is far up on your leg. I'm sorry, okay?" His tone was rough.

"Alright. Me too. I'm not used to people taking care of me."

"So, I noticed. I also detected a few other things about you."

"Oh yeah, like what?" Her mouth curved into a smile.

"I can almost bet you had some training on medical emergencies." He lifted an eyebrow at her.

"You're right." She laid her head down on her arms folded under her head, her auburn hair splayed out over her shoulder.

"Before I started looking for Rose, I was a nurse in the pediatricians' hospital."

"Do you miss it?"

"Yes, but nothing I can do about that now."

"Is your boss aware of what's going on?"

She sighed before answering. "John told me to take a leave of absence and not tell them about searching for my sister. The concern was the possibility of losing my job, and I would have a hard time getting another one in that area."

The mention of Lancett's name put a bad taste in Craig's mouth.

"Does Lancett control your every move?" He spoke before thinking, realizing too late as Susan's back stiffened.

"No, John does not tell me what to do. I trust his judgement is all."

If she knew the real John Lancett, she would not trust him at all. This reminded him.

"What does your father's company deal in?"

"Papaver somniferum," she said relaxing a bit. "Why?"

Craig paused for a minute. "That is illegal to produce in United States."

"Not if you're cultivating the plant for the poppy seeds." She battled back with a pompous tone.

"How did your parents come to be involved in those?"

"My mother had a fetish for poppy seed. She loved it on lemon cakes, bagels, and even as an oil. One of her favorite dishes was Poppy Seed

Roll. My father cherished my mother so much he decided to make a living out of them."

"You are aware of what else that plant is used for." He had hoped his affirmation was not insulting to her.

"Of course, I do. That is why the DEA does their inspections of the orchards every so often."

"Which is more than likely why the drug Cartel wants their claws on your parents' company. They would obtain the main ingredient to produce the heroin the DEA is trying desperately to eradicate off the streets." Disgust hit in his last words.

"Has anyone ever tried to buy your father's business?"

She paused for a moment before answering. "If my memory serves me right, I recall one night overhearing my mom and dad talking about some guy named Jerry De something wanting to purchase it."

"Jeremy DeVore?"

"Yes, that is the name. Do you know him?"

Craig closed his eyes. He was afraid of that. DeVore was one of the lead men for the drug Cartel. They would want the outfit for the opium to manufacture their heroin.

He opened his eyes up to Susan's head turned in his direction with the deer-in-the-headlight stare.

"What is wrong?"

"Does Lancett possess the ability to sell your father's corporation?"

"No, I do. Why?"

"Good, because I have a strange notion about the whole case." He did not elaborate to her.

"How's your leg? Think you'll be able to walk around in a grocery store?"

"I guess. How does it look?"

Craig carefully removed the ice pack from her thigh and checked it over.

"It's fine. We need to be going." He took off for his room and finished getting ready.

* * *

Susan recognized the blue Sedan parked by the house next to the one they were occupying.

"I see your friends are staying at your uncle's house."

He glanced in the direction of the cottage and nodded.

"I guess you are blessed with a lot of acquaintances around here."

"Yep."

"Can any of them help with finding Rose?" She was ready to get the all-out search for her sister moving.

He hesitated for a moment before speaking.

"There are a few people out here on the trail."

"Great! Where do we start?"

"At the grocery store. Need our energy for this, don't we?" She caught sight of a halfhearted smile from him.

The building was smaller than what she shopped at in the city. Brand names were scarce throughout the store.

They came to the bakery where Susan hung around eyeballing the baked goods. Some donuts, along with Mexican pastries, lined shelves behind two small Plexiglas doors which swung open. She scanned the different kinds of treats before deciding on her favorite. Cream filled scones.

She looked around for Craig, but he had moved on. Going down the aisles with her bag of sweets, she spotted him talking to a woman.

The woman appeared to be in her late twenties, light brown curly hair, and slim. Glasses she wore made her appearance more appealing than of an ordinary Jane. The mystery woman glanced in Susan's direction, and then nodded at Craig. When Susan neared them, she overheard the other woman telling him she would meet him before the Days at The Bays weekend festival.

Craig gave his full attention to Susan as his friend left down the aisle.

His face was hard. Had she interrupted something between them two? Were they setting up a date?

"There are a few more items to pick up." His voice was stern. She could only nod.

Chapter 18

On the ride back to the house, Susan mulled over to herself. There she was in the company of a man she knew little about. He was an undercover drug enforcement agent carrying a gun, which could be extremely danger-ous. She put a lot of trust into this man who had a year earlier threatened her life because she found his ledgers leading to a narcotic bust. What did she step into?

Craig said he had told John where they were, but she would call him on her cell phone telling him exactly her whereabouts. She did not like him controlling the whole situation and calling John a criminal.

Passing by the lighthouse RV park, she noticed the same vehicle from the day before where some men had been gathered around a map. All but one man dispensed into different cars and took off, leaving the one at the camper. She considered checking out the men. Might not be anything, but everything to her was worth investigating. Including the woman at the store Craig talked to. Not that she was jealous of the other woman.

A gunshot rang out as they pulled up to the house. Craig uttered some-thing under his breath and told her he would be right back as he headed over to the other cottage, leaving her with the key to the house.

She took the groceries inside and went to her bedroom to call John. She paid close attention to the sound of the door opening, alerting her to when Craig would come in.

"John?"

"Susan! I have been worried sick about you. What is going on?" He was livid.

"Well, I got a lead on Rose."

"Why didn't you tell me? Where are you? I'll come for you now."

"I need to stay where I'm at. She's not too far away."

"How do you know?"

"From the blue notebook. Cr-."

He interrupted her. "You found the folder? Fabulous. I'll be there shortly." He hung up before she said anything else.

Craig must have told him where they were because he did not give her time to tell him. Did she dare tell Craig she had called John, and he was on his way down?

The front door opened, and she quickly put her phone back in her purse. She came out of the room and asked what had happened.

* * *

"Those guys were being prevented from going down the steps by a rattler. After they shot it, they argued about who was going to go down first. They are afraid of a dead snake." He chuckled to himself.

"So, what did they do?" He noted her innocent face.

"I dragged the serpent off." He answered her question with his mind elsewhere.

"That was nice of you."

"Nice?" He focused back to their conversation.

"Oh, yeah. I guess. Couldn't leave them stranded upstairs. They would starve." He smiled with the thought of the two men having to explain to their boss why they were unable to keep tabs on Craig and his *lady friend.*

"What would be funny about leaving them hungry?"

Susan was serious. He had to stop and think for a minute.

"I wasn't smiling about that. I was thinking about having a dead snake blocking the only access down from the house and overcoming the fear of snakes."

"Or intensify it more. Incidentally, I overheard your friend at the store saying something about a carnival?"

"Sergeant Garcia? Yes, she did. The festival is held once a year to celebrate the bodies of water. It consists of a few rides, and each night a different band is on stage. The marina transforms into a sandy dance floor at night."

"What does this have to do with finding my sister?" Susan folded her arms in front of her and raised her eyebrows at him.

"Plenty." He brought out the blue folder, opened to a certain page, and placed it in Susan's hands. "Read." He pointed to a starting point.

"It says the Rose will be traded off at the celebrations of the waters. Okay, so when is this happening?"

"This weekend." He gave her a wide grin, pleased they were making head way sooner than he had expected.

"That's three days away! What do we do until then?"

"Actually, two. It starts on Friday night. So, we wait."

"Alright, Craig. You wait. There are a few things I'd like to look into while you're waiting."

"What do you plan on looking into?" He did not want her to do anything to bring attention to them. They needed to keep a low profile until they found Rose.

"You don't worry." She darted off to her room and back out with her purse when he caught hold of her.

"Where do you think you're going?"

"To check on something."

"How are you going to get there?"

"You have cabs out here, don't you?" Her eyes blazed with discontent.

The town had one cab which would come out that far, but he did not want her to go off by herself. Especially with the danger waiting for her.

"Please, let's work on this together. No matter what you think, I do care about finding your sister for more than on the egotistic side."

She hesitated for a moment. "At the lighthouse beach something appeared out of the ordinary. Some men were around a map on a table."

"What's so strange about that? Plenty of tourist have those."

"Well, these guys weren't your regular travelers. They wore business suits."

He rubbed his chin for a minute before speaking.

"Let's go. I'll meet you downstairs. I need to make a phone call first."

* * *

Moments later she lowered her window down taking in the air her lungs had begun to accept. The odor became something she could adhere to. Her favorite part was the breeze slapping her in the face, blowing her hair into the wind. A feeling of freedom.

A freedom Rose was not enjoying. Guilt washed over her, and she raised the window back up.

"Haven't gotten used to the smell yet?"

She glanced over at him. "Yeah."

They approached the causeway; she kept her eyes peeled for the camper she had seen with the men hovering over the map. A few vehicles pulled out, then she spotted it.

"There," she said pointing at the RV coming out of the park. "Follow them."

"What?" Craig eyed her in dismay. "I'm not going to trail them without a good cause. It is not worth getting us shot at. We'll just come back later and find out what's going on."

He turned the car around and headed back to the house. She was furious at him for not following the vehicle. But as bad as she hated admitting it, he was right. They would probably land themselves into trouble and not be able to help her sister.

"Looks like a storm is brewing in." Craig spoke up. "These storms off the bay are the worse. They come upon you quick and heavy."

They drove a couple more miles before a torrential downpour came. She could hardly see in front of her and wondered how he spotted the road. Tension shown on his face as he maneuvered through the rain.

The run up the stairs proved fatal. They still managed to end up drenched. Susan rushed into her room to shed out of the wet clothes, but not before grabbing a towel from the bathroom.

Craig was already sitting in the living room when she came out of her room. Her hair was damp with drops of water occasionally dripping down her shirt. The yellow tank top she wore exposed chill bumps on her skin. She flopped down on the couch facing the TV and crossed her arms trying to keep warm.

"So, what's on?" She tried to sound casual.

"News," he responded back.

The weatherman said a tropical depression had blown in around two o'clock. With every strike of lightening came the unmistakable roar. She had never been in a house that shook with the thunder.

Craig told her not to worry, it would pass. "The worst that can happen is the electricity go out."

As if on cue, the sky lit up and a loud crack sounded. The television tube popped and went out, along with the lights.

"That's great! Now what do we do Mr. Voodoo?" Sarcasm hit in her voice.

"Sit back and wait for the power to come back on."

"In the dark?" Even though it was mid-afternoon, the heavy clouds caused the skies to go black as night.

He chuckled. "If you're afraid, I have some lamps in the other room."

He left her on the couch, and she responded to his last statement.

"It's not that. I just like to see what's going on."

He came back in carrying a lamp being careful while putting it down on the small coffee table in front of her. He opened a little drawer in the table and pulled out a box of matches. After lighting and adjusting the wick, he tossed them back in their place. Susan caught sight of some pho-tographs tucked in the back.

Her curiosity peaked up. "What are those pictures of?"

"What pictures?"

She retrieved the photos. "These."

Craig was propped up against a tree with a brunette woman sitting between his legs leaning back into his chest in one. In another one he and the brunette were kissing. Jealousy started rearing its ugly head but was snatched away along with the snapshots.

"None of your business." He took off for his room with his pictures clutched in his hand and slammed his door.

Susan sat dazed for a while trying to figure out what just happened. The thunderstorm outside was mild compared to the one that had hit within.

Chapter 19

Had Craig not known the lay out of his bedroom, he would have stumbled over everything in the dark making his way to his nightstand. He retrieved the flashlight from the drawer and stood it on its end. The light hitting the ceiling gave him sight into the room.

He sat on the side of the bed staring at the pictures he grabbed out of Susan's hands. The pain and memories of Lillian flooded back to him. She and their unborn child were taken from him. He would not forgive whoever was responsible for their deaths.

He could not even excuse himself. They were gone. Now he had to go on living without them and help other people. That was the oath he took. And in the other room sat one person he vowed to assist. Susan.

Upon opening the door, he found her where he left her. He emerged from his room and walked over to the couch, standing for a moment in front of her. When she lifted her head to look back at him, pain stabbed his heart. How could he hurt her the way he did? She was going through enough problems without him adding more. He perched on the coffee table facing her.

"I'm sorry for getting upset at you."

"That's fine." Her eyes swollen with tears shimmering in them. He cursed himself for causing her pain.

"No, it is not. You did not deserve the way I talked to and treated you. You are entitled to the truth. Those photographs are pictures of my wife, Lillian. She was pregnant with our child. The crib at my grand parents' home was for him. Unfortunately, a couple of years ago she was killed before she gave birth."

Susan reached out to him and encompassed his hand into hers.

"I am so sorry Craig. I did not know." Susan's eyes filled with compassion.

"I know you didn't. Hopefully, you can help guide me to the people who murdered her. They have something to do with the disappearance of Rose."

"Why do you think that?"

"Lancett told me when I hired you, you were the one to lead me to the killers. The only way I conceive that happening is by finding who kidnapped your sister."

The lightning struck and the thunder roared, informing them the storm was not over yet.

Susan let go of his hand. Her eyes as wide opened as her gaping mouth. "I just don't understand what John has to do with all this."

"What part does Lancett have in your parents' company? And why aren't you or your mother the president?"

She hesitated for a moment, and then let out a sigh. "My mother was killed in the airplane crash with my father, and I didn't want the headaches. I'm sure your next question is going to be somewhere on the line of 'why let John Lancctt run the company?'"

"That would be it."

She got up from the couch and paced the floor between it and the dining room table a couple of times. After the second trip toward the table she turned around and stopped, bracing herself against it. Her attention averted elsewhere as she spoke to him.

"He worked for my parents for ten years. My father, Frank, considered John the son he never had. Showed him all the ropes to the firm, inside and out, and doted on how fast he was learning. No one else fitted the role better than him."

"Does he have all the say so other than not being able to sell it?"

"No, and that is one place he and I would argue about. I retained the corporate function of CEO in absentee."

"This meant he couldn't do anything with the company without your say so."

"Correct." She set her mouth in a hard line.

"If you trusted him, why not turn everything over to him?"

"My mother was in doubts about him. She said my father was too hyped up on the idea of having someone interested in the business he overlooked some things."

"As in what?"

"Overindulging into his budget for one. Dad would toss it off as being young, and he needed more than what they allotted him."

"What else?"

"My mom felt John would sell it if he got the chance to."

"Why did she think so?"

She shrugged her shoulders. "She didn't say, but that was mainly why I didn't give him the full run of the place. Frank and Francis Mullican worked hard building that company, and I did not want to be the reason why it got sold. I'm already the cause for one tragic accident."

"What would that be?"

A loud boom of thunder rolled in the distance. The storm moved away from them, but darkness still loomed.

She sighed before answering him. "I'm responsible for my parents' plane crash."

The news Susan gave him was surprising. "Oh, and how so?"

"I was studying nursing in Louisiana. On my twentieth birthday I wanted my parents there. They said they had a business trip to Tahiti they needed to make. Something about a transaction to take place. I persuaded them to come visit me. They never made it. The engine on the plane failed, and they crashed shortly after taking off. It was my entire fault. If I hadn't been so self-centered, they would still be alive."

Craig perceived she tried to be strong, but a teardrop slid out. He cautiously walked over to her. Her eyes glazed over, and her chin quivered.

With his thumb he gently wiped away the tear. On impulse, he took her into his embrace. Her body shook as sobs silently escaped her lips. What could he say to ease the suffering she was going through?

* * *

Susan could not believe she told him about her parents' plane crash. Yet she did, and now she was crying in his presence.

She could not help it. She held the pain in for so long, and he offered her the strength she needed through the remembrance of that fatal day.

"Craig, I'm sorry."

He smoothed out the back of her hair. "Don't worry, sugar," he told her. "Not your fault."

She drew her head away from his shoulder and blinked through the tears. He looked down upon her face.

"Why do you say that?"

"The engine failed when they took off from home, so it wouldn't have mattered where they were going. The plane still would have crashed."

Susan stood for a moment digesting what he just said. Other people mentioned the same thing, including John, but her brain never registered it until Craig said it. Perhaps she was ready to accept the truth. And she could not think of anywhere else she wanted to be at that moment besides where she was. In his arms.

The rest of the evening whirled past her. She vaguely remembered eating dinner Craig made, then each heading off to their rooms for the night.

* * *

Susan thought she was dreaming when she realized someone was knocking on her bedroom door.

"Yes," she rang out groggily.

Craig opened the door and moved inside the room, positioning himself close to the entryway.

"How did you sleep, sugar?"

"Fine, I think," she replied.

"There are two more days before the festival, and I have a few things to do." He gave her a smile, then turned towards the hallway.

What did he need to do? He had not mentioned anything to her before. She scrambled up out of her bed before he left the room.

"What's the plan?"

He spun around. "You are staying put," he told her.

"What? I don't think so. My sister is out there, and I want to be abreast about what's going on."

She crossed her arms in defiance.

He gave her a once up and down. "I'm sorry but I can't take you into the police department."

"Why not?"

"We are trying to protect you, and sometimes it is best if you stay away from what's going on. You will be safe here. My two friends will see to it."

"How can I depend on them when they're scared of a dead snake?" reminding him of the day before.

Craig cracked a smile with a small sound of a laugh. "I promise you, sugar, this is the best place for you."

He swiftly headed off into the other room.

Susan took off after him but did not catch him before he closed the door to the restroom. She tried to put a lot of trust in him, but some things she was not sure of. Like his friends next-door. Are they people who would not harm her? And was the woman at the grocery store in fact somebody on the law side helping them?

Two feelings struck her at once with the last question. Jealousy of the other woman, and the emptiness she felt inside without her sister.

She could not sit and do nothing while Rose was somewhere close by. She had to do something.

Susan waited until Craig came out of the bathroom when she hit him up.

"Please let me go with you?" She pleaded with him.

"I told you it would be too dangerous for you to be out. We took a chance going to the store yesterday. We were lucky Lancett, or whoever is behind Rose's kidnapping, didn't run into us."

"Well, if John's a criminal as you think he is, I doubt if he'll be going to the police station." Let him make an excuse out of that, she thought to herself.

His features softened.

"Alright, but you must stay in the lobby."

Satisfaction overwhelmed her.

"I'll give you some time to get ready, but please hurry. It is imperative I meet with Sergeant Garcia here soon to go over the plans."

"I will, I will!" Susan ran into her room and grabbed some clean clothes before taking off for the bathroom.

Her mind raced around about finding Rose, that her shower took her five minutes in and out. She did not want to give him any reason to leave without her. She was not thrilled about him meeting with Sergeant Garcia, but if it brought her closer to a breakthrough, she would manage it.

Craig was on the phone when Susan came out. His eyes met hers, and he immediately ended his call.

"Are you ready?" he asked as he picked up the keys off the table.

"Hold on. I just got to grab my shoes."

She rushed in her room and hurriedly retrieved her sandals while tossing her worn clothes on the floor by the bed. Hurrying back into the living room, she threw them down and slipped her toes between the straps.

"I'm ready."

She smoothed out her sundress where it ridden up from her dashing around. A smile emerged from Craig as he opened the front door for her.

Outside the sun hovered above the bay, giving it the shimmering silver affect. Other than the damp ground, no signs of the thunderstorm which blew through the night before existed. The docks lined with people fishing up and down.

Instead of turning right like they did the day before to go to the grocery store, they went straight. Susan spotted the marina as it appeared in front of them, along with a couple of rides.

"Is that where the festival will be held Saturday?"

Craig nodded his head. "It starts Friday night, tomorrow, but we will be more interested in what happens on Saturday."

He turned right and added "I don't think it will be safe for you to attend."

He glanced over at her with a hint of intensity.

They parked in the back. Soon they rounded to the entrance. Red bricks saddled the glass doors leading into the station with an emerald-green dome. The badge right below the top displayed a star in the center. Above it the words announced Port Emerald. Police hugged the foot of it.

Once inside, Craig ushered her to the lobby where chairs lined a wall as he stepped to the window asking to speak to Sergeant Ginger Garcia. Susan studied the woman as she came out the side door in a police uniform. She acknowledged Susan with a nod, then directed Craig through the door.

Susan picked up a magazine from the table by her chair, and aimlessly thumbed through the pages. She did not like the fact that she was uninformed about finding her sister while Craig was in the back with... *Ginger*...doing whatever. Were they even discussing the case? Or playing detectives?

She tossed the magazine back in its place, and almost jumped to her feet. The lady officer behind the dividing plexiglass wall gazed in Susan's direction. Susan smiled at her, and the officer gave a curt smile before dropping her attention back to her paperwork.

Susan paced a couple of times. Her mind was grabbed by an activity on the other side of the street where a small café with outside seating stood.

A group of men were perched on the seats enjoying their meal and drinks. Upon closer inspection, she recognized one of the men as an employee who worked at her father's corporation. She checked out each man's face in case she identified anyone else. The man on the end was no other than John Lancett.

He did say he knew where she was. How long had he been here?

John laughed at something. He turned his head, and his eyes hit the windows of the police station. His smirking faded and a spine-chilling look replace it as he stared into the building.

Susan felt her blood drain out of her face. She instantly turned her back to the window in hopes he had not seen her. The side door opened, and Craig waltzed out. After eyeing her, he stopped.

* * *

The meeting with Sergeant Garcia for their next move for apprehending the kidnappers went well and ended on a good note. Until he stepped out into the lobby, and Susan looked like she had seen a ghost.

"What's wrong?"

Susan vaguely got out John's name when Craig peered behind her at the café across the street. Five men hustled to leave, and one of them resembled Lancett.

He observed which vehicle they climbed in. It was a white Jeep. More than likely a rental because of the license plate. They took off toward the outskirts. A few hotels were in that direction. If Lancett was staying in town, he would be hanging out in one of those.

"He's gone, now. Did he see you?"

He noticed Susan's color coming back, but her lower lip trembled.

"I-I'm not sure. He must have because he took off pretty fast."

He drew closer to Susan, and cautiously guided her to the car.

"I still have a couple of more things to do, but first I'm getting you back to the house. I don't want to take any more chances of meeting up with Lancett with you in tow."

"Wait a minute! I am very much capable of handling myself."

Susan glared at him so hard he felt the heat on the side of his face.

"You didn't appear very capable back at the police station," he batted back at her.

"I was just shocked, that's all. I recognized one of the guys with him. He works at my father's corporation as well."

"What about the other three?" His detective mode kicked in.

She shook her head. "No, I am not familiar with them."

"I have to ask you a question, and I need the truth. Have you been in contact with Lancett recently?"

She did not respond. Her silence gave him the answer he needed.

"Okay," he started. "At least we know how he found us."

"What do you mean?" Susan fumed. "You informed me that you notified him where we were."

After a bit of hesitation, she blurted out "So, you lied to me?"

"Yes," he admitted to her. "Which means if you didn't tell him, and I didn't, he is the one responsible for Rose's kidnapping." He gave her a long side glance. He wanted to watch her reaction to the revelation dealing with Lancett. She looked about as white as she did when he came out of Sergeant Garcia's office.

BAM! BAM! BAM!

"What the...!"

Craig swerved out of control, causing the car to go into a ditch.

Chapter 20

Susan gripped tightly to the dash as the car jumbled and jarred around in the ditch. They came to an abrupt stop. Letting out the breath she held in through the rumble tumble, she asked Craig what happened.

"Seems someone's not happy we're here. Or they're making us aware we are being watched."

They both piled out and checked the backside of the BMW. Three holes plummeted into the trunk. Craig's jaw strutted out baring his teeth.

"The miracle is they didn't hit anything major."

Craig regained his composure. "I'll notify a tow truck to pull us out of this gutter. Afterwards, we should head back to the house." Upon his last note, he pulled out his phone and made the call.

They stood on the border of the meadow when help arrived. A big burly man stepped out of the cab. His face was familiar to Susan, but she could not place him.

"Stuck in the ditch, hey?"

The man rubbed his chin which had what appeared to be years' worth of hair growth.

"Yes," Craig answered back. "I'm hoping you can eradicate it out, so we can be on our way." Tension held in his voice either from the situation they were in, or the senseless question the man asked.

The man grunted. "I'll see what I can do."

The man eyeballed Susan as he moved to the back of his wrecker and brought out some heavy-duty chains. Within minutes, he hooked the cables up to the front of the BMW. The equipment on his vehicle dragged the car back on to the pavement.

While Craig paid for the tow, Susan realized where she saw the man before. She stayed calm so he would not know she recognized him.

"Thank you, sir. We appreciate your help."

The man nodded leaving a leering gaze at Susan. He jumped up in his cab and took off down the road.

Craig inspected his car as she made a chilling statement.

"That guy sat at the table with John today." Her voice quivered a bit.

A blank expression came on his face. "Are you sure?"

She nodded. "Yes. I checked him out while he was pulling up the car."

His face hardened. "Alright. The car's drivable so let's hurry back to the house."

They both hopped in and sped off.

After pulling up under the house, he tossed Susan the keys. "I'm going over to talk to Kelley and Maxwell. I'll only be a few minutes."

She observed him quick stepping over to the other house before she climbed the red stairway to the awaiting deck. She lingered awhile facing the bay, taking in its beauty.

An unfamiliar sound caught her attention. She peered off to her right. At the back of the house she spotted two pieces of an aluminum object. A head crowned, and a face appeared. He was the tow truck man.

She opened her mouth to scream, but the man promptly displayed and pointed a gun at her. Fear replaced the grin on the man's face as the ladder pulled away from the railing. A rustling sound, and an audible "ugh" came from the ground. Susan ran to the end of the deck. Down below, the three men had the intruder captured.

Craig gazed up at her. He said something to the two men before taking off around the side of the house. She hustled to the landing where Craig scaled the stairs to meet her at the top.

"We will not be safe here. A secure hide-a-way is close by. You will need to shut your phone down, so we are not tracked there. Grab your things, and we'll head out in twenty minutes."

Susan nodded and closed down her device. He held out his hand for it. She was compelled to protest but decided to give it to him and gathered her belongings together.

"The place we're going," he explained as he maneuvered through the twist and turns of the road, "is closer to town, but still off any major roads. It is a two-bedroom small farmhouse. Kelley and Maxwell," he glanced into the rear-view mirror at the Sedan following them, "will be staying with us for protection. You will still have your privacy in one of the rooms. This should all wrap up in a couple of days, if not sooner. Afterwards you can get back to a normal life with Rose."

The last sentence dropped off a bit. Susan thought she detected a hint of sorrow in his voice. As crazy as it sounded, she almost did not want the time with Craig to end. But she knew he was right. They met under precarious circumstances, and each had their own lives they put on hold to find Rose.

They turned off the street they were on and drove on a scarcely used dirt road. The grass was sparse in places and tall bushes approached them fast. Craig kept going straight towards them, and Susan wondered if he was going to stop.

She braced herself for the impact just as they hit the shrub. They went through them, but it did not affect the vehicle like she thought. She gave him a very perplexed glare.

"Where we went through at is not a hedge. However, the other hedges you see are real. Helps keep out unwanted guests." He chuckled.

In front of them a small house stood covered with live oak trees. An enormous door swung opened, and they pulled into a deep garage with the two men behind them. The door closed, and an interior light came on in the room.

"This will be home for a couple of days," Craig announced as he got out of the car. All four of them removed their bags from their vehicles. The side door into the house led them into a quaint kitchen.

Her attention was grabbed by the small windows with metal bars in front of them as she studied the room.

"What do you do in case of a fire?" She bobbed her head towards the windows.

"There is a release latch on the inside," Tony volunteered the information.

"Permit me to formerly introduced you. Ms. Mullican, this is Tony Kelley, the youngest of us." Tony nodded his head. "And Randall Maxwell is the old dog of the company."

"Watch it, Craig. You're no young pup yourself." Randall ribbed him with his elbow. "Nice to meet you ma'am."

"Like wise." Susan directed her next question to Craig. "So, what's next on the agenda?"

The three men eyed each other apparently keeping a secret between themselves.

"For now, why don't we settle into our rooms, and eat a little something? I'll show you to yours."

Craig helped her with her luggage. He took the lead through the house to a small room and deposited her belongings just inside the doorway.

"The bathroom is down the hallway. I will be staying in this room next to yours. The two guys will be alternating shifts and utilize the couch in the living room."

Craig's expression softened as he came closer to her. He affectionately glided a stray piece of hair on her forehead over to the side, and traced her face with his finger, landing under her chin. Tenderly he raised her face, studying her for a moment before speaking.

"I am not sure of what to expect this weekend. All the law enforcement here and around the vicinity are working on finding Rose. I want to keep you safe and away from any harm. I want you to remain here at the house with Kelley and Maxwell tomorrow night. Can you do that? Please?"

"Craig, you have no right to tell me I cannot go. My sister is out there!"

* * *

There it was. That stubborn chin strutting out. How was he going to knock through her thick skull the danger they were in? He dropped his hand from her jaw and rubbed the back of his neck, trying to relieve the headache coming on.

"This is going to be risky for me to be seen at the festivity. Lancett's *goons* are shooting at us, and now we are moved to a hide-out because they followed us to my place. I just can't take the chance of losing you."

Did he say that? Did he mean it? They have spent a lot of time together, and it had been quite intense. He could not believe those reasons would override his feelings.

"Lo-losing me? What are you saying?" She struggled with her words.

"Do you remember in the blue folder the part about plucking the pedals of the rose and the sweet smelling red one?"

She nodded her head, and her shoulders slumped a bit.

"I'm sorry, Craig. I guess I'm just so wound tight that I want to find Rose and wake up from this nightmare."

A tear escaped Susan's eye. With a subtle move of his thumb, he carefully wiped the moisture away.

Yeah, he meant what he said. He did not want to lose her. Still, he knew their time was coming to an end.

"We'll find her one way or another. That I promise."

Craig went to his room and unpacked the necessary items he would need for the next couple of days leaving the rest still packed.

He met her at her doorway, and they both made their way into the kitchen area. The square baking dish containing the enchilada bake was the center piece of the table which sat all four of them with ease.

"It looks and smells delicious," Susan complimented Tony.

He blushed a bit as he thanked her. "It is a recipe that's been in my family for years."

They all scooped out some enchiladas as well as some beans and rice.

"So, what's the plan for tomorrow, Craig?" Randall questioned as he shoved a forkful into his mouth.

Susan eyed Craig intently but still maintaining her apparent appetite for the delicious meal.

"I talked with Sergeant Garcia today. She said they acquired information of where the trade will be taking place, but they're still working on where Rose is being held at."

Craig shifted his eyes to Susan. He was not sure what kind of reaction he was going to encounter from her. She slowed down her chewing and swallowed the food in her mouth.

"Where do they think the tradeoff will be?" Susan spoke up.

"They believe it will be at a nearby airfield."

"Oh, yeah," Randall chimed in. "How far away is the airport?"

Craig brought his attention back to Randall. "It is about thirty-five miles north of here by La Mere. There is no place to dock a boat there, and it doesn't coincide with what the paper said inside the blue folder."

Tony raised his brow. "What did the article say?"

"Port Emerald was mentioned as well as the craft, but the police department came up empty locating it on the marina. Perhaps it is coming in later."

Tony pulled out his cell phone. "What's the name of the ship? I will see if a buddy of mine can locate it. He's fantastic about finding vessels."

"Queenboat 947."

Susan dropped her fork and the color drained from her face. Her mouth gaped open as a sound barely came out. Everyone focused on her and ceased what they were doing.

"What's wrong?" Craig was startled.

"Queenboat 947 was my father's plane that crashed."

She abruptly got up from the table. Craig followed her to her room and closed the door after entering.

Susan's back was to him. Her body shook from sobbing. He compassionately turned her around and wrapped her up in his arms. She willingly accepted his actions and wept even harder in his embrace.

He kissed the top of her head and held her even tighter. Susan's weeping slowed down, afterwards stopping. She squinted up at him, and his heart melted. How could he ever think this precious soul was involved with the drug Cartel?

"I'm sorry, Craig. I have been trying so hard to be strong for Rose ever since she disappeared. Guess I'm losing it."

"You don't need to apologize. I am the one who needs to ask for forgiveness from you. I put you through some tough times you didn't deserve, because I thought you were linked to the Cartel."

"Here I was thinking you were dealing drugs because of those ledgers I found in your offices. It was hard to trust you."

"You had a good reason not to. Especially after I threatened you, which I am so sorry for."

"I forgive you, but I can't John for what he's doing." A sob escaped her lips.

"I think we should tell Kelley and Maxwell everything is fine. What do you say?"

* * *

She agreed with Craig.

Embarrassment invaded her self-esteem. For a second time she found herself blubbered all in Craig's chest. That is not the way she had envisioned being in his arms.

The two men understood her leaving the table in a rush.

"Look, missy," Randall began, "don't worry about excusing off your actions to us. We're rough guys, but ones with a heart." He gave her a wink.

"I have an idea of how we can scope out the dance tomorrow night, and not be recognized," Tony asserted.

"How so?" Craig asked.

Tony picked up the small local newspaper off the coffee table and brought it to the kitchen. He opened the paper up to a page about the upcoming Days at The Bays Weekend Festival.

"The article states on Friday night they are having a masquerade party. I can go into town tomorrow and buy us some masks." Tony gleamed.

Craig and Randall stared at each other. Craig responded. "It could work. I'm still not completely at ease about Susan going." He set his eyes on her.

"I promise I will not give you any problems." She needed his approval to go to the event. As much as she would like to go searching on her own, she knew she would be safer with the three men.

Craig hesitated for a moment before agreeing to her going. "Please stay close to us."

"I will. Thank you so much."

"It's getting late, and I think Susan and I should head to our rooms for some rest. Have you two decided who is taking first patrol?"

"Tony's going to get some shut-eye first since he's going out first thing tomorrow to find those masks. So, I'll make me some strong java. See y'all in the morning."

Everyone said their good nights, and Randall turned to the coffee pot.

Susan grabbed a pair of night clothes along with her robe, slippers, and night case then headed toward the bathroom.

She took a hard assessment at her reflection in the mirror. The search for Rose had taken a toll on her. Not once did she think about lines on her face because of her young age. Now she is seeing some popping up on her forehead. Worry lines as her mom would call them. She longed for her parents and the carefree life they all had. Even though Rose was a pesky little sister at times, she missed her.

The tears started streaming down her face again. When she reached for some toilet tissue, her toiletry bag tumbled over to the floor making a loud clanking noise.

"Are you alright?" Craig's voice echoed from the other side of the door.

"Yes, I'm fine. I knocked over my case." She tried hard not to sound like she was crying. He witnessed her weakness earlier that day, and she did not want to give him a reason to back out of her going to the festival.

He replied 'okay', and she heard him go back into his room.

"Get it together, Susan," she silently told herself.

She finished up her nightly routine and settled into the twin bed. Her body was ready for sleep, but her mind stayed wide awake. While going over the day's events in her head, what stood out most to her was the realization her judgement of John Lancett proved to be wrong.

Her mother did not trust him, and Susan was glad now she retained the firm in her possession instead of handing everything over to him when her parents died.

Craig said John was involved with the drug Cartel, and the plant her father's corporation grew was the chief ingredient for heroin, as well as other drugs. She wondered if her father thought about that when he first started the company.

Her thoughts went to what lay ahead of her, and what will she discover at the festival? All hopes and prayers were to find out where Rose was being held at.

Chapter 21

Susan woke up sore all over. That was the first time she remembered sleeping on a twin bed. A good thing the bed rested up against the wall, otherwise she would have fallen off. Instead, she bumped into it a few times in the night. Once, hitting her head, and Randall knocked on her door checking on her.

She fumbled for the clock on the end table which displayed seven o'clock. She drugged herself out of bed, put on her house shoes and housecoat, and shuffled her way into the kitchen. The aroma of the coffee lured her to the fresh brewed pot. In the cupboard she found a mug and poured herself a cup, then sat down in a chair at the table.

The side door leading into the garage opened. Craig and Randall walked into the room. They stopped their talking when their eyes met Susan.

"You appear to be a little on the rough side," Craig spoke. "Was your bed comfortable enough?"

That did not boost her self-esteem. "You know how to make a woman feel desirable," she tossed back at him.

Randall nudged his elbow into Craig. "You need some lessons on how to talk to a lady, mate."

"I'm sorry. I guess what I meant is you seem a little run down."

Randall elbowed him again, and Susan raised her brow at him.

"I need more coffee," Craig settled on saying, turning to refill his cup.

She glanced around the kitchen. "Am I the last one up, or is Tony still asleep?"

"Na," Randall responded. "Tony's gone to the local department store to purchase us some masks. He should be back soon. I'll be glad too. My eyes are ready to view the backside of my lids." He gave out a small chuckle.

Craig's phone rang. Looking down at the caller, he quickly answered. "Hello Kelley." A brief silence. "What do you mean they're out of masquerade masks?"

Craig stayed quiet, but his expression displayed his discontent for the conversation.

"Any place else you can go to?"

Susan and Randall sat patiently waiting on Craig's reply.

"I see. Well I guess the festival is off tonight. We cannot show up without masks, or we'll definitely be spotted by Lancett and his gang. Sergeant Garcia and her people will be our ears and eyes. Come on ba..."

"Wait!" Susan shouted.

Craig jumped and almost dropped his cellphone.

"Tell him to go to the arts and crafts area. I'll relay to you what he needs to grab."

"He heard you. I'm going to give you the phone and you can instruct him."

She nodded, taking the device from him.

"Hey, Tony."

"Hi, Susan. Give me a couple of minutes. I'm sure I'll need a cart."

"Yes, you will."

Craig expressed a concern. "Are you experienced in making masquerade masks?"

"Yes. Remember at your house I told you I worked as a nurse in the pediatrician's hospital?"

"Yes."

"One day for fun us nurses and the children made some. We had a little party and wore the ones we made."

"You do realize these are for grownups, right?" His forehead puckered.

Randall gave him the elbow again. "You don't learn, do you? Give the lady credit."

Susan suppressed her temper. "Of course, Craig. We wouldn't want you looking like a clown, now would we?" She smirked.

Randall howled, and slapped him on the back. "I guess she can stand her ground. Have to with you, Summers."

A small chuckle sounded over the line before Tony announced he was ready for her list.

"First, we need a package of crafting foam sheets. If you can find one with different colors, would be excellent."

"Found one."

"Search out some elastic string. Something we can use to hold the masks on our faces."

"Got it."

Susan pressed her lips together for a moment while in thought. "Some designs come to mind, so go over to the paints and pick out a gold color, turquoise, orange and black. Also, a bottle of paint thinner and an assortment of brushes."

While Tony searched for the colors, she inquired of the two men if there were any decent scissors in the house. Randall inspected the kitchen drawers while Craig explored the living room. Craig came back in holding a pair.

"Will this work?"

Susan grasped them and found a piece of paper to try them on.

"Yes, these will."

Tony came back on the line informing her he found the colors.

"Next check if they carry colored feathers."

"Yes. Any colors in particular?"

"Aqua, white, and black."

"Done."

"Lastly a hot glue gun and sticks. That should be all we need. I'm going to hand you back over to Craig. Thank you, Tony."

"You're welcome, Susan."

"We'll see you back here soon. Good-bye." Craig closed his phone, then turned to Randall.

"Maxwell, if you want to go ahead and rest before the night, you are more than welcomed to sleep in my room. We will be fine."

He graciously took up Craig's offer, and headed towards the room.

"I guess I'll hit the shower. It is going to take me a while to make all the masks." She downed the last bit of her coffee.

"Can I speak to you for a moment?"

"Yes." *Oh great!* He is going to tell her she is not going. Well, that is not happening. She is going.

"I'm sorry for offending you this morning in front of Maxwell. You really don't look bad. In fact, you are kinda cute. Like a rag doll." He smiled and straightened up her housecoat.

She gave him the evilest eye possible before storming off to her room. At least he did not try to talk her out of going to the festival that night.

* * *

Craig stood dumbfounded. "Now what did I say?"

He shook his head, grabbed the laptop from the living room and placed it on the kitchen table. Searching through the local airport logbook on the government site, he typed in Queenboat 947.

The plane landed a couple of days ago. The expected date and time of departure were the next day at four p.m.

"Darn it!" Craig spat out loud, hitting his fist on the table.

"What's wrong?" Susan came into the room with her hair damp from the shower.

He hesitated for a moment before giving her the news.

"Sit down please."

She sat down in the chair left of him.

"I researched your father's plane in the airport site, and it came up."

Her eyes were as large as her grin. "That's good, right?"

"Yes, and no," he told her. "The scheduled take off is tomorrow at four in the afternoon."

Susan's mouth gaped open. "Oh, no. That doesn't give us much time to find Rose."

"This evening the Harbor Master should have the vessel she is being held on pinned down. He's been working on this case."

The side door opened, and Tony came in carrying bags.

"I stopped off at the deli and got us some lunch meat, cheeses, and bread. Figured we might want to keep our strength up." Tony's boyish grin showed off his dimples.

"Just like you." Craig chided. "Always thinking about your stomach. How do you stay so slim?"

"It's all about the core, my man." Tony gave a wink.

"A couple of more bags are out in the car. If someone could grab them, I would appreciate it."

Tony deposited the sacks on the counter while Craig exited to extract the other ones.

Craig opened up the back door on the passenger side when something caught his eye. He went to the back of the vehicle where he saw an indent. White paint was pasted on top of the blue color inside the cavity.

He grabbed the bags, shut the car door, and entered into the kitchen.

"What happened to the Sedan?" he questioned Tony.

"What do you mean?"

"A dent is on the passenger's rear panel. Evidence of a white vehicle hit you."

Tony took off into the garage with Craig on his heels.

Tony scratched his head. "I didn't witness that. The incident must have happened while I was in the store."

"We can't notify the insurance company here. We will wait until this case is over and inform them back at the base. To cover your tail, put it in your report."

They headed back into the kitchen where Susan searched through the items purchased.

"Hey, I'm going to start on the masks." She collected what she needed and took off for the living room.

Craig surveyed Susan as she laid out the materials in order. For the first time she showed contentment. The project gave her something other than worrying about her sister to focus on.

He settled back down to the laptop on the kitchen table. Tony busied himself with the sandwich makings. The scenery was more like an everyday occurrence instead of three people, four if you count Randall sleeping, hiding out to stay alive, so they can find a young lady who got caught up in some sick drug Cartel game.

At least he learned why they kidnapped Rose, and why Lancett wanted to acquire the sisters' company.

Tony brought the sandwiches to the table along with some bottles of water.

"Lunch is ready," he announced.

"You sure eat early," Susan spat out from the living room.

"You never know when the next time you're going to eat a sensible meal in this business." Tony justified his position.

"This is true," Craig agreed, snatching up a sandwich and water. "You better get you one before we devour them all up."

"Alright." She pulled herself up from kneeling at the coffee table. "But after we finish, I need Tony's face."

Tony's expression was almost distressed. Craig chuckled.

"I have this beautiful cockatoo mask in mind for you. We'll put the feathers up to emphasize your stature."

"My what?"

"How tall you are." Susan gestured with her hand above her head.

"Oh. What about Randall?" Tony bit into his sandwich.

"A wise owl. His gray hair highlighting his waves will look awesome."

"I hate to ask what your plans are for me." Craig uttered.

"For you, a raven. Bring out your masculinity." She put emphases on the last word.

"Why do I need a mask for that?"

"You don't. It seemed appropriate for you." Susan took a swig of water.

"What about you, Miss Mullican. What are you going as?" Craig teased her a bit.

"A bluebird."

"Why that bird?" Tony asked.

She shrugged. "They're my favorite."

The three of them consumed the rest of their meal in silence. After they finished, Susan grabbed Tony by the hand, leading him over to the couch and sitting him down. She picked up a white foam sheet and wrapped it around his face lengthwise.

Craig glanced over while she made some marks on the soon-to-be mask where Tony's eyes would be, then brought his attention to the laptop. He had some more work to do before the festival later that day.

He punched up the marina on the government site, checking out all the vessels docked there. Jack Sprinter was the Harbor Master, whom he had associated with for several years. Craig vacationed in Summersville for the summer right before starting the police academy when Jack first came on board in Port Emerald. Jack was a person he trusted to find out where Rose would be held at. He had a reputation of making sure nothing peculiar went on at his docks.

Randall emerged from the bedroom and bellowed out a hearty roar. Craig steered his eyes to the scene which caused Randall's laughter, and could not help but chuckle at the mask Susan made for Tony. The white feathers were pointed straight up, and the nose spiked downward.

"I wouldn't laugh, Randall," Tony warned. "You're going to be a wise *old* owl. Although wise, I am not sure about."

"An owl?" Randall said in disbelief.

"Yes, and I'm about ready for you."

Susan finished adjusting Tony's mask on him.

"I got to pour some java in me first, missy."

"Well, Craig," she turned in his direction. "I guess you're next."

Randall came into the kitchen. "So, what are you going to be? A cuckoo bird?" He let out his robust laugh.

"No. A raven," Craig returned.

"Why? Because you hunt down your prey?"

"No. To bring out my masculinity."

Craig pushed himself away from the dining table and headed over to Susan. Randall was having fun with Craig's answer.

"You are relieved of your duties, Mr. Kelley. I will take over from here."

Craig filled the empty spot once occupied by Tony. "Let's get on with this."

"It's quite painless," she informed him as she reached for a black sheet. "Sit still while I wrap this around your face."

The intensity in Susan's expression as she brought the fabric up to his face burned in his mind as the blackness from the material invaded his sight.

"Now I need you to hold this on your face while I mark where your eyes are. You might want to close your eyes while I do this."

Susan guided each of his hands up to the side of the foam. The warmth of her hands comforted him. Her compassion overwhelmed him at times to a point of wanting her as his soul mate.

Nevertheless, he knew how she felt about guns. He also carried a deep scar from what happens to the family of a law person. He could not forgive himself if something happened to her because of the line of work he had chosen.

Susan lowered the sheet, and a baffled expression came over her face. "Are you alright?"

"Yes, why?"

"You look like you lost your best friend. I didn't hurt you, did I?"

"No, you didn't. Guess I was thinking about tonight." He gave a weak smile.

"Me too. At least making these masks helps the time go by."

Craig detected a glimpse of sorrow in Susan's eyes before pepping herself back up and continuing on with the design of the raven.

Randall moseyed over to Susan, watching with intent as she cut around the eyes with care. "So, what are you going as?" he asked.

"A bluebird."

"Any certain reason why we're all going as birds?" Tony asked.

"Birds of a feather flock together," Randall scoffed.

Susan stopped what she was doing and gazed up at Randall. "I have not thought of it like that, but that phrase has a proper ring."

She motioned Craig to her as she put the foam material up to his face.

"This Days at The Bays is a celebration of the bodies of water, correct?" Susan stated more than asked.

Craig nodded in response.

"Well," she began as she brought the mask to the coffee table and arranged some black colored feathers on the face. "On the fifth day God also created the birds when he made the living creatures from the waters." Susan started hot gluing the feathers as she finished up speaking. "I figured it would be better to make us bird masks versus water inhabitants like squid, shark, blow fish, and mermaid."

She held up the raven mask checking out the detail work she had done.

"I wonder who would have been the blow fish," Randall elbowed Tony.

"More than likely you with as much hot air you discharge," Tony threw back.

"Yes and no," Susan spoke out. "I'm ready for you, wise owl." She put the raven mask beside the cockatoo and searched through the package retrieving another white foam sheet.

Craig and Randall switched places.

"So, missy, why would I have been the blow fish?"

Susan gave him a big smile. "Because of your wavy hair."

"I guess I didn't see that coming," Randall cracked.

The place erupted in laughter. Craig gave Randall a gentle tap on the back before returning to his laptop on the kitchen table.

* * *

Susan was glad for the distraction. She wondered what life would be like after they found her little sister, and they returned to East Texas.

John would wind up in prison for this stunt. Rose would take his place with the running of the company since she gained more knowledge about the business. Susan would stay in the medical field.

Then there was Craig. She had to admit to herself about her feelings for him. Would this be the kind of life she would endure with him? Hiding out from criminals who want you dead?

Dead! Oh, no! What if they do not find Rose? Or worse yet, what if she has been killed?

"You okay, missy?"

Susan blinked back some tears which escaped her tear ducts.

"I'm sorry, Randall. I guess I strained my eyes too much."

It was a half lie. She could not tell them the real reason.

All three men were watching her.

Craig moved from his chair in the kitchen and came over to her.

"Would you like to take a walk outside with me? I need to stretch my legs for a bit."

He held out a hand to her, and she took it, grateful for the break.

"Don't wander too far," Tony cautioned them as they headed toward the side door.

They exited out the back of the garage through a metal door. The sun on Susan's face was a welcoming warmth to the chill the air held.

They walked about midway of the length of the house when he stopped.

"We might want to stay in this area. This way Maxwell and Kelley can keep us in their view."

Craig pointed to the window where the two were keeping watch. They nodded at Craig, and he returned the nod.

"If the search for your sister is getting too much for you, I can arrange for you to be safely taken away and back to your home."

His expression was deep. She could not determine if he wanted to be rid of her, or if he was concerned about her. Either way did not matter to her. She was going to follow this to the end, and be there when, or if, they find Rose.

"I appreciate it, but I can't leave. Not when we are this close. I hope you can understand." She pleaded with her eyes not to send her home.

Craig let out a heavy sigh. "Again, I don't know what we'll find. I pray God we find her alive and well. From what I have encountered regarding this particular drug Cartel, the turnout is not always favorable."

A sudden and hysterical tapping on the glass startled them. When they stared in the window, Tony pointed out to the field while Randall ran to the kitchen.

They turned their heads in time to detect a white vehicle with dust billowing behind, headed toward them at lightning speed. A loud bang rang out, and Craig drew Susan to the ground with him, covering her with his body.

Chapter 22

Randall crawled towards Susan and Craig with his gun drawn. "You two okay?"

Susan sensed security in Craig's arms, and calmness in the scent of his Stetson. Nevertheless, she peeked out from under his protecting body. "Are they still coming?"

Craig pulled his handgun out of his belt behind his back. He and Randall ventured their heads above the bushes veiling them. Tony came out, shoving his pistol in his holster inside his jacket.

"It looked like a truck full of early party goers for the festival," Tony proclaimed. "They turned with the bend in the road. I'm sure the bang we heard was a backfire from the vehicle."

The two men made their way up to a standing position, and both helped Susan up from the ground. All three of them brushed the dirt off themselves.

Craig put his hands on his hips. "I think I stretched my legs enough. Did you take in enough fresh air?"

"Yes. There is a bit more to do on Randall's mask. Afterwards, can you help me with mine, Craig?"

Susan usually does not ask for assistance with projects like this, but she wanted to linger in Craig's company a little while longer. She now knew what her dreams meant in the year before they hooked back up together at the last bargain store. He was not a callous person. At least, not to her.

He winked at her. "I look forward to it."

They moved back inside. Tony started cooking while Susan continued with the owl. Craig stood beside her.

"I'm sorry I doubted your ability to make these masquerade masks. You are a highly creative person."

"Thank you, Craig. That means a lot to me coming from you." Susan glanced up at him flashing him a sideways grin.

She carefully stroked the final touches of gold paint to the owl and placed it with the other two. She reached inside the package of foam sheets and pulled out a light blue one.

"Are you ready to help me?"

"You bet."

"Sit here please." Susan patted the sofa cushion next to her. Craig vigilantly came from behind the couch and sat where she indicated.

"I'm going to wrap this around my face. I need you to take the marker on the coffee table and mark where the center of my eyes is at. The same way I did you earlier."

Susan put the sheet up to her face. She knew their relationship had grown, holding more trust in him not to hurt her.

A little pressure came from the felt tip pen, and Craig asked if he pushed too hard.

"No. Did you do it?"

"I'm hoping I did it right."

She took down the foam and turned it over, looking where he made the dots.

"Perfect," she said with a smile. "I'm going to fix up the bluebird and should be done between fifteen and twenty minutes."

"Excellent," Tony called from the kitchen. "Dinner will be ready as well."

"I don't have an idea of what I'm going to do once this is over. I'm not used to someone else cooking." Susan gave out a chuckle. Tony's boyish grin surfaced.

Craig's mouth displayed a half smile, but his eyes showed sorrow.

"Is there anything else I can help you with?"

"Yes. Would you please search through the feathers and pull out all the aqua color ones you can find?"

Craig nodded, then focused his attention to the task given him.

While cutting the design of the mask, she wondered if he would miss her after this assignment was over.

She still remembered the times they had over a year ago before their relationship went sour. More of that affection returned.

Susan felt duped. She suspected Craig was involved with dealing drugs. All along it was John. And she assigned him in charge of her deceased parents' company. If she had only taken the time to learn the business, she might not be in this predicament.

"That should be all of them, sugar, uh Ms. Mullican. Sorry."

She gazed up at him, and he motioned with his eyes toward the two men in the kitchen. She took the gesture as he did not want them to be aware of their affiliation, giving him a knowing nod.

"Alright. I have a few more things to do to the bluebird before I am done."

"I have a couple of things to do as well before supper," Craig said as he vacated his seat.

* * *

That was a foolish slip of the tongue, Craig scolded himself. He did not want to give Tony and Randall any reason to believe there was a conflict of interest with this case.

Although certain Susan was innocent concerning the Cartel, for the sake of the government he still had to treat her as a suspect. Especially since she told him her parents firm dealt in the growing of papaver somniferum. Better known as opium poppies. Number one ingredient in heroin.

He trusted the Mullicans were only interested in the plants for the poppy seeds. It is unfortunate they hired a snake like Lancett. He would not be surprised if he had them killed so he could take control of the orchards. Thankfully, Susan had a sound head on her shoulders. Keeping Lancett from making any decisions on the sale of the business was smart.

The uncertainty of how far Lancett would go to take over the company faced them. He hoped they would find Rose unharmed. His memory of the carefree young lady from the store a year ago played in his mind. God would have to intervene in order for him not to do away with Lancett should any harm come to her, or Susan.

"Dinner is about ready."

Tony's announcement brought Craig thankfully out of his thoughts. He was getting all worked up, and he needed to keep his head straight for the escapade that night.

"Talk about timing," Susan exclaimed from the living room.

"Got it done, missy?" Randall asked.

"Yes. Now the glue has to dry. By the time we finish eating it should be ready to wear."

Randall gave out a whistle. "Some of them fillies at the carnival are going to be green with envy."

Susan and Randall joined Craig at the table. Tony deposited a delicious looking Shepherd's Pie dish in front of them.

Susan's eyes widened. "Wow! You really can cook."

"Thank you. My grandmother raised me to learn how to fend for myself."

Tony passed around the salads. Afterwards, he took his seat at the table.

"I definitely can't complain." Randall drummed his stomach. "While we're chowing down, Craig, we need to go over our plans."

"My lieutenant, Dan Johnson, made it into town. He's been meeting with some of your FBI guys at the RV grounds."

Susan broke in. "Do you mean the men I had been telling you about at the park are part of FBI and DEA?"

Craig nodded.

She pointed towards Tony and Randall. "You two are federal agents, not drug enforcement?"

"Yes," the two men said in unison.

"Why are both agencies on this case?"

Craig answered her question. "Because I can only address the narcotic trafficking going on. The FBI can investigate the kidnapping since it is related to the Cartel."

"Plus, any other calamity that crook struck up." Randall added with distaste in his mouth.

"That is well-organized the two governments working together. So, there is no need for the local police?" Susan asked.

"On the contrary," Tony responded. "All three of the government offices work as a group at times. Sergeant Garcia and her unit has been a tremendous help."

"Yep," Randall engaged. "Ginger is a real sweetheart."

"She helped us consult with some locals among other things," Craig piped in.

"Yeah, who would want to talk to a bunch of stiff necks and renegades they didn't know." Randall ended with a snort.

"True," Craig replied. "When we arrive at the fairgrounds, we'll seek her out. She rounded up a couple of people you and Kelley can interview. I will confer with the harbor master. He had been working on a list of possible vessels Rose Mullican may be held on."

"What about me?" Susan inquired. "What do I do?"

If Craig had his way, she would be staying at the house with the two agents guarding her. That was not an option. Time continues to run out on them, and he needed all the help he could wrangle.

"You and Sergeant Garcia will be keeping your eyes and ears open for anything suspicious." He felt secure leaving her with Ginger. Ginger was one heck of a wild cat. The two ladies together would be able to hold their own.

The four of them finished up their meal. Susan volunteered to clear the table and start the dishwasher. Out of courtesy, the men geared themselves up with guns and handcuffs in the bedroom with the door closed.

"You know I'm not too crazy about missy going, don't you?" Randall directed his statement to Craig.

"Truth be told, I'm not either. But whoever is going to make the trade for Rose Mullican is going to do it tonight or in the morning. The plane she will be on is taking off tomorrow afternoon around four."

Tony let out a sigh. "Not much time. Let's hope we find her tonight."

"A good praying would help," Randall voiced as he slammed his revolver inside his boot.

Craig and Tony agreed.

The three men exited the room. Craig scanned the living room and kitchen for Susan, but she was nowhere in sight.

Chapter 23

The bedroom door to the room occupied by Susan opened. She came out wearing a blue summer dress with buttons on the front and a matching shawl.

Randall let out a whistle. "Aren't you looking pretty, missy."

"Thank you, Randall. It will go perfect with my bluebird mask." Susan's smile diminished. "If only this was a celebration instead of a search party."

"Don't worry, missy. We'll find your little sis."

"I know you will." Susan reached up and gave him a kiss on the cheek.

She grabbed the masks off the coffee table and handed each man their mask. "White cockatoo for the tall and slender Tony. The wise owl for the eldest of the group. And the raven for the masculine man." On impulse, Craig gave her a wink.

"Let's get this show on the road." Randall snatched up the keys and took off through the side door.

Randall stopped short of inside the garage and peered toward the back end of the vehicle. "What in blazes happened to the Sedan?"

Tony quickly answered. "Someone must have hit me while I was in the store."

"I'd say they did, and a heck of a job at that. They left some white paint on the corner panel." Randall shook his head as he rounded the car and entered the driver's side.

Tony climbed in the front while Craig and Susan settled into the back. He turned around and asked Craig if he wanted to sit in the passenger seat.

"It will be better if I'm back here in case Lancett or one of his people happen to drive by us. They will recognize me, and I don't want us targeted."

He nodded before turning back around.

"You said they were in a white jeep?" Randall took a gander in his rear-view mirror at Craig.

"Yes, and more than likely a rental. I couldn't catch the name of the company on the license plate holder, but I'm sure it's one in La Mere."

"Makes sense," Tony put in. "Lancett probably rented a car there after landing the plane in their airport."

Dusk approached them as they drove over the causeway. The small town came into view with a few lights lit on the outskirts. The marina, however, was shining bright, and people were on the Ferris wheel. The music boomed louder as they arrived at the festival.

"I think we should go ahead and put on our disguise." Everyone agreed with Craig and positioned their masks on their faces as they came to a stop. Randall guided the Sedan into the parking lot, maneuvering in a slot by a dumpster.

"Might not be the best smelling thing to park by, but at least we know where we're parked at."

"Remember to stick to the plan. Any problems don't hesitate to call me." Craig looked at Susan. "You will be with Sergeant Garcia while I'm talking to the harbor master. If anything happens, she will be in touch with me. I'm sorry we can't take the chance of Lancett homing in on us through your phone."

Susan gave a knowing nod.

* * *

The small group exited the car, and together went in search of Sergeant Ginger Garcia.

Craig spoke up. "Sergeant Garcia told me earlier she would be around the merry-go-round about this time. She said she would be wearing a peacock mask and a colorful outfit. I think I spot her."

Susan could only envision Craig's face because of the covering, but she was almost certain he was elated at seeing Ginger. Once she laid eyes on the other woman, she understood why. A gorgeous peacock mask adorned her face. Susan felt like an ugly duckling.

Ginger acknowledged the four of them, then proceeded filling them in on people to talk to.

"Tony Kelley."

"Here," he answered.

Ginger smiled. "I like your masque. A cockatoo, right?"

"Courtesy of Miss Mullican," Craig shot in.

"They all look fantastic. Did you do them all, Susan?"

Heat inflamed on Susan's cheeks. She had not expected a compliment from her. "Yes, yes I did."

"What a wonderful job. Anyways, Tony, one of the crew members of the barge boat docked in lot fifty-six on the Dry Bulk Dock is in possession of some information relevant to the case. His name is Drew Smith. He will be expecting you at the teacup ride. He is wearing a stork mask and about your same height. Should be easy to find him."

Tony nodded.

"Randall Maxwell."

"Hoot, hoot," Randall chuckled.

"Wise owl," Ginger grinned. "I like it. You will be meeting with Toby McAbee. He runs the airport in La Mere and said he would be happy to talk to you. There are a couple of suspicious planes which flew in a few days ago. I believe one of them is Queenboat 947, the one which is the main interest. He's over by the shooting gallery in a falcon mask."

Randall nodded, and he and Tony took off in the directions of their destinations given to each man.

"Craig, Jack Sprinter is in his office. He's waiting on you and pinpointed a vessel used to hold Rose Mullican."

Ginger took a long survey of Craig. "I like that raven mask on you."

"Brings out my masculinity," Craig teased.

"Like you need *that* to bring it out." Ginger gave out a snicker.

Susan was not at all amused at them.

"While I'm gone to visit Sprinter, will Miss Mullican be out of harm's way with you?"

"Oh, yeah. My radio is on, so I will be able to keep up with what is happening. All my people are on duty tonight, so they should not need me, unless an emergency pops up. In that case, I'll appoint an officer to stay with her."

"Sounds good. See you ladies later." Craig gave Susan a lasting glance. Almost like he did not want to leave her.

But he headed off toward the Pier Terminal Building leaving her with a woman whom she happens to be in competition with.

"We'll find your sister. Between the FBI, DEA, and our law enforcement we've managed to put the details together of what the drug Cartel plans to do."

"Have you known the men long?" Susan's focus was more on Craig and Ginger's relationship, but she did not want to come off as a jealous woman.

"Craig, yes, but not the other two. I have heard about them, but that's about all."

"How long did you know Craig?"

"We grew up together. That is every time he had come to Port Emerald. When my grandfather came here as an immigrant from Spain, he left my grandmother and my father to search for a better life for them. Craig's great grandfather took him in under his wings and helped him. Our families blossomed an everlasting bond together since then."

"That was charitable."

Ginger kind of laughed. "Charity didn't have much to do with it. Back in the sixties when the hurricane took out most of Port Emerald, my grandfather worked to help put this town back on its feet. Mr. Summers held the chief of police office here at that time and saw how hard he labored. He trained him into the law enforcement agency, assisted him in becoming an American citizen, and brought my relatives over. Out of gratuity to Mr. Summers, my family remained here to sustain this community."

Susan was awed by the story told, but her underlying question still did not reach an answer.

"So, you two are close?" The question busted out before Susan caught it.

Ginger gave her a knowing wink. "We are like brother and sister. I am happily married with two sons. Craig is part of our family as we are his."

She looked around in the crowd, then smiled. "See the man with the two boys by the ring toss booth?"

On cue, the man turned his head in their direction, and waved. Ginger waved back. "That is my husband and boys." She displayed pride in her voice, which made Susan seem small that she acted on jealousy towards this woman.

"They appear to be having fun. Do they ever worry about you in this line of business?"

"Every time I step foot out of the door."

Ginger's radio awakened. "Sergeant Garcia, you are needed in the restroom area. An unidentified male is knocked unconscious."

"Roger that," Ginger responded back.

"Officer Callahan," Ginger called to the patrolman coming up to them. "Would you please stay with Miss Mullican until Craig Summers, or I come back?"

"Yes ma'am."

As soon as she left, Tony came up to Susan. He grabbed her hand and told her Craig needed her. Officer Callahan asked for the man to remove his mask and to show some identity. Susan told him everything was alright, the man was Tony Kelley, an FBI agent.

He rushed through the crowd while holding tight to Susan's hand. A couple of times she almost tripped. She yelled at him to slow down, but the noise drowned her voice. She clung on firmly to her shawl to keep it from sliding off her shoulders.

Tony drew Susan to the parking lot. Once there, she surveyed fervently for Craig. She pulled her mask off to gain a better view of the area. The lamp lights through the foggy mist of the evening did not help her much with her vision.

"Where is he? I don't see him."

The eerie silence coming from Tony brought her attention to rest on him.

"I wish you searched for me the way you do Craig, sweetie."

The tone was harsh, and definitely not Tony's voice. But 'sweetie' was John's nickname for her.

She gazed in horror as he slowly took off the disguise. When he uncovered his face, he was John. Her breathing became shallow as her chest hurt from her heart beating so hard against it.

"Wh-where's Tony?"

"He's sleeping, just like you're about to do." A sinister smile exploded on John's face as she felt someone behind her put a cloth over her mouth and nose.

The scent on the fabric held a definite odor like her parents' plant, but stronger. The stench gagged her. She reached up to take it off, but the person compressed the material further up her nostrils. She took in one more breath before her body went limp, and she blacked out.

Chapter 24

Craig rushed to make it back to Ginger and Susan. The information Jack gave him pointed to the barge in lot fifty-six. The same one Tony was to meet with a crew member off of.

When he arrived at the location which he left the two ladies at, they were not there. Instead, he encountered a lawman.

"Excuse me officer?"

"Officer Callahan. May I help you?"

"Yes. Do you know where Sergeant Garcia and a young lady named Susan Mullican, who was with her, are at?"

"I relieved the sergeant while she went to check out an incident which occurred around the lavatories. And an FBI agent, Tony Kelley, came to take Miss Mullican to Craig Summers."

Craig rubbed the back of his neck. "I am Craig Summers. Can I speak to Sergeant Garcia?"

The officer's eyes widened. "Yes. Hold on."

He picked up his radio and talked into it. "Sergeant Garcia, come in please."

"Garcia here," came the response.

"Craig is here. He wants to talk to you."

"Put him on. Craig, we have Tony here in the parking lot. He's being attended to by the E.M.T. Someone knocked him out behind the restrooms."

"Is he in possession of his mask?"

"No, that is missing. However, a stork one was found close by."

He let out a heavy sigh. "Alright. I'll call Maxwell, and we'll meet you there."

"Roger."

Craig's gut wrenched as he hurried to Ginger. Randall would join them after his interview with the owner of the airport in La Mere.

Tony jumped out of the ambulance as Craig arrived on the scene. "Is Susan with you?"

"No. Officer Callahan said she left with you to take her to me."

"That was not me. I met with Drew Smith at the teacup ride. He said he wanted to talk somewhere in private. We walked to the back of the restrooms, and I got hit in the back of the head. He must have taken my mask. I'm sorry."

Craig shook his head. "It is not your fault."

A car moved past them. The headlights exposed something peculiar in the parking lot. Craig motioned to Tony and Ginger to follow him. On the ground laid Susan and Tony's masks along with Susan's blue shawl.

"Darn it!" Craig clenched his fist.

Randall ran up to them. "Where's missy?"

"Taken," Tony responded. His shallow tone echoed Craig's feelings inside. He had to find Susan.

"I'll grab some men to mark off and work this area and see if perchance the incident was caught on film." Ginger motioned with her head at the camera above them.

"Where is the monitor at for this one?" Some hope shone through the darkness for Craig.

"Back at the station."

Ginger radioed for a team out to the scene. "I'll meet y'all there," she told the three men as they hurried toward the Sedan.

Craig hopped in the front passenger seat, and Tony clambered in the back. Randall blasted the car down the street.

"What did you find out from the airport owner, Maxwell?" Craig needed to keep his mind busy. He did not want to ponder on what could be happening to Susan.

"Seems our John Lancett flown in on Queenboat 947 with a pilot a couple of days ago. But he is not leaving out on it tomorrow. Toby spoke to the operator, and he is only aware of taking some fillies back with him to Dallas."

"Must be the two sisters he will be escorting. It does not make sense. Why go through all this trouble to draw them here, and later take them back up?"

"Who knows the mind of a drug dealer," Tony remarked.

Randall parked in front of the police station. All three men jumped out of the vehicle and made their way into the building.

A uniformed lawman met them in the lobby and ushered them to a back room.

"We scanned over the tapes and found what we believe to be the female victim and her assailants."

Assailants? Meaning more than one person attacked Susan. Craig tensed back up and messaged the back of his neck trying to loosen the knot forming.

The officer turned on the video. The clip displayed a horror scene unfolding. Susan was being pulled by her hand into the screen by someone who was wearing Tony's mask. She looked for something in the lot. Probably for Craig since that was what she was told. A few seconds later the man took off his disguise.

"Stop right there," Craig barked. "Can you capture a closer picture of the man's face?"

The officer zoomed in on to the person's face. Lancett revealed a sinister facial expression.

"Darn it!" Craig hit his fist on the table. "Sorry," he immediately apologized.

"No need to be. Shall I continue at normal frame?"

Craig nodded.

He observed another person coming up behind Susan and put a cloth over her mouth. She struggled and before long went lifeless. A white jeep pulled up and stuffed her in it before taking off.

Something strange about the vehicle caught Craig's attention.

"Can you back up the frame to when the jeep comes into view?"

"Yes."

"Can you zoom in on the left front bumper?" Craig strained to get a better vision.

"That is the color of my Sedan on the bumper," Randall roared.

"So, they marked the car we drove." Tony twisted his lips.

"Which must be how they knew what masks we wore. They staked us out." Bitterness hit in Craig's gut.

"That is all we caught of them. We have put out a bolo on that jeep. We will add the paint on the front fender to it. Most of our people are out at the festival, but I had been in touch with the FBI. They are keeping their eyes opened as well." The officer clicked off the video.

Sergeant Garcia entered into the room. "Were you able to identify who kidnapped Susan?"

"Yes. John Lancett. The same person we believe is responsible for kidnapping her younger sister, Rose Mullican." Craig anguished at the thought of Lancett taking those two ladies for the sake of their parents' company. All over drugs.

"Did Jack have any leads, Craig?" Randall inquired.

"Yes. He's more than positive the person from the barge Tony was going to question is where Rose Mullican is being held at."

"That vessel," Ginger put in, "has been here a few times. It belongs to a poppy seed grower's company. They paid off a couple of our people to let them pass through. We're certain drug activity is going on."

"That ship must be our target. Didn't you tell us Susan's parents grew poppy seeds?" Concern laced Tony's voice.

Craig nodded. His mind whirled around ninety to nothing on devising a scheme to rescue the two women.

"You got something going on inside that brain of yours, mate. Let's have it." Randall was intent on Craig spilling his next moves.

"I don't have it all worked out yet, but it will take all three departments for the plan to work."

Ginger eagerly informed Craig she and her force had his back. Tony and Randall followed right behind with their allegiance.

* * *

Susan woke up to a thumping noise ricocheting in her head, giving her an excruciating headache. Unable to move her hand to the pain, realization set in that they were tied to the bed above her head. She tried to move her feet, but they were secured with rope as well.

Groggily she adjusted her sight. She was in some metal building but could not figure out where the banging came from. Turning her head to the right, she detected someone in a cot across from her. Rose. Her shimmering blonde hair now a matted pile of strings.

"Rose!" she wailed out. Rose turned her head and blinked a few times.

"Susan! Oh, my gosh. I thought it was you they dragged in, but I wasn't for sure."

"Did they hurt you?" So many questions she wanted to ask her little sister, but Rose's physical condition was at the top of the list.

"Not really. Only tired of being bound up like an animal."

John's voice echoed through the building as he came out of the shadows, startling both women. "Won't be too long now, Rose, and you will not need to worry about being bound up again."

"John, what got into you? You're supposed to be our friend." Susan choked back some tears forming. She could not believe he actually stooped this low.

John gazed at her with an ominous smile.

"This could have been avoided if you would have only married me, Susan."

He came closer to her, stopping inches away. He took a tin case out of his pants pocket, opened it, briefly dipped his finger in it, snapped it closed, then dropped it back into his trouser.

Her skin crawled as he lowered himself over her and attempted to rub the substance on her lips. She turned her face before he made contact. He forced her head back up by her chin.

"Don't resist me!"

With his hand still on her face, he pried open her jaw by squeezing on both sides of her cheeks with his fingers, and at once jammed a finger down her throat, gagging her. He rubbed something awful tasting all in her mouth, mostly scraping the upper side.

Susan squirmed with all her strength against him. Even tried biting him, but for some reason her muscles in her face started tingling. Soon, a funny feeling took over. He drugged her with something foreign to her. Her body did not respond to her commands.

John disembarked from her. An evil smile danced across his face. "Now, that's better. Heroin isn't too bad now, is it?"

He groped over her with his eyes.

"My, such a beautiful sundress. You always did dress sexy."

He sat down on the side of the cot by Susan's knees. Without warning, he reached up and unbuttoned her top button, startling her.

"Do you know how many times I dreamt about undressing you?" His eyes blazed with a craving that scared her.

"Leave my sister alone!" Rose sobbed.

John stood, turned toward Rose, and strode the short distance to her cot. Susan was so numb all she could do was scream out in her head while her voice strained against its cords making little noise. Tears once held back streamed down her face.

"Do not be concerned, Rose. I am not going to hurt your sister. I have other plans for her. For both of you." He turned his attention back over to Susan.

"I hate to leave such good company, but I have a show to put on. I'll be back after a while to bring you two up to the main act." John gave out a small grunt adding, "If you regain your voice back, Susan, use it wisely. If you scream, it will just sound like seagulls from the outside."

He smiled then exited out the door.

"Don't worry, Susan. The effect of the drug doesn't last too long. I just pretend like it does, so they don't keep shoveling the nasty stuff down my throat as much."

Oh my God! They drugged her little sister for a year.

"I'm sure you're wondering what happened to me," Rose began. "It's still kinda fuzzy, but after so long of playing over in my head, I can see most of the scene as clear as if it occurred yesterday." She let out a heavy sigh.

"I went to work one day, and Danny, my boyfriend there, who I didn't tell you about, talked me into going into the back room. When I went in the back, I couldn't find him. He crept up behind me and gave me a deep French kiss. I felt strange afterwards."

Susan laid stunned by what Rose told her. Recapturing the incident of John plunging his finger into her mouth, releasing the heroin at the back of her throat.

"Well, my boss told me to go home, and Danny volunteered to take me. I dropped down in the backseat of his car. The next thing I knew I was tied up in this barge. Later I found out it is the one mom and dad used to ship the poppy seeds across the waters in."

That explained the banging Susan heard when she woke up. Water lapping at the bottom of the barge.

Barge! Susan remembered Tony was going to talk to someone who worked on one. Maybe the same one. Surely hope for the two of them to make it out of this alive existed.

Chapter 25

Craig followed Sergeant Ginger Garcia as she led them to the barge located in lot fifty-six with their guns at their hips, ready to pull and use in an instant. A few of her officers marched with them.

He knew he was taking a chance of Lancett being on the ship, but he wanted to lay eyes on Susan himself. The video of her being snatched in the parking lot continually played over in his head all night.

Gazing down the pier at the two-story boat, he did not detect any movement aboard. All hopes were Lancett had not transported the sisters to the airport yet.

Upon closer inspection, he observed a motion on the top deck. He tapped Ginger's shoulder and pointed. She fastened her eyes to the direction indicated and nodded.

As Craig, Ginger, and the officers proceeded closer, a man about five foot seven inches with brown hair, and clean-shaven, emerged from a door in the bottom cabin. "Can I help you?"

"We were informed you have drugs aboard. May we inspect the vessel?" Sergeant Garcia addressed the man.

The man gave a cocky smile. "All we carry is poppy seeds, and she's empty at this moment. One of your dock workers took the remainder off yesterday of what we had. Didn't you read the logbooks?"

Jack Sprinter told Craig the night before the barge unloaded some product, but not as much as their usual shipment.

"Less than your normal load," Ginger replied.

The man shrugged. "Orders have been down." He rubbed his chin for a few seconds. "Yeah, if you want to look at our books, that's fine." He motioned for them to come aboard.

Craig, Ginger, and three of the officers with them jumped up on the deck, following the man inside the cabin. Four men sat at a table. One of them spoke to the man who had been talking to them.

"What's going on, James?"

"Not much, captain. It appears when business is slow, you're accused of carrying drugs." The men all laughed, causing an uneasy air.

The captain stood. "So, we're shipping narcotics, are we? Why are you so sure of that?" He pointed his gaze at Craig.

Craig spoke up. "Our sources told us the company you're hauling for is using some of the poppy seed plants to make heroin. The duty of the DEA is to check out any and all transactions this business makes. Including shipments."

"So, what do you want from me?"

"We need to examine your logbooks and inspect your cargo hold."

The captain raised his brow at Craig's request. Behind the ship master, the four men became a little restless. Craig prepared himself for a fight.

"I'll show you my logbook." He maintained eye contact with Craig while telling James to fetch his records from the top deck. "You'll see, Mr. DEA, that I'm legit."

A few seconds passed before James came back downstairs with a book which he handed to his boss. After opening to the transactions made the day before, the captain placed it in Craig's hand with a crooked grin on his face.

Craig studied the record for a minute before handing it back.

"It appears to be in order. Now if you would be so kind to show me to your cargo hold, we can conclude our investigation." Craig gave him a broad smile.

Craig was more interested in seeing below deck. Should Susan and Rose be on the ship, that would be the most likely place they would be held at.

 TO FIND THE ROSE by Sara Kendall

"There is no need to check out the storage, my friend."

Craig veered his attention to the direction the voice came from. Lancett came up the steps.

"Why not?" Craig questioned him.

"Nothing is down there, I assure you." Lancett produced a wicked expression. One Craig did not trust.

"I am still required to audit it." He held firm with Lancett. He put his hand over his pistol on his side, steeling himself to draw.

Lancett's smile faded into a snarl. The men on board jumped to their feet in a menacing way. Craig quickly drew his gun, along with Ginger and the officers with them. Craig kept his weapon pointed on Lancett.

"Well," Craig began. "I had hoped this was going to be an easy day, but I guess not. So, Lancett, are you going to show me what's below deck, or will one of the shipmates?"

Lancett gave a sinister laugh. "My, are you mistaken, Summers. It hasn't even begun to turn hard on you. Yet!" He growled out his last word.

Lancett's men pulled their guns out and aimed them at Craig.

"Looks like we out number you, DEA man." James displayed a dark and proud smile. "Six to five. I like them odds," he jeered.

"Actually, it's more like ten to one," Lancett announced.

Ginger gave Lancett a knowing nod, then she, along with the three officers with them, turned their weapons in Craig's direction.

"Sorry, Craig," Ginger said apologetically. "Our town was sinking financially. The drug money is what kept us afloat."

She disarmed Craig from the pistol in his hand and gave him a nudge with her gun to his ribs. He raised his hands up for her to pat him down, taking his other arms off him. Ginger retained her gun on Craig, while the others put theirs away.

Lancett beamed with delight. "Beneficial to us, the Port Emerald police are bought off. Thanks to Ginger and her people, I knew to expect you. They also informed me the FBI left for La Mere in hopes of catching the plane before taking off with two women. Rose and Susan." He glared at Craig.

Craig maintained his coolness to Lancett, but his insides continued to churn. He was only ninety percent certain the ladies were still on board the ship.

"I always had my suspicions that you work for the DEA, Summers. Even though Mike Holmes was a corrupt cop, he would never give you up. You do remember Mike Holmes, don't you?" Lancett's eyes narrowed.

"Yes," Craig replied. "He works in the missing persons' division."

Lancett raised a brow. "You mean worked in the missing persons' division. He mysteriously became one of the missing." Lancett waved a hand in the air, snickering.

"Imagine being a dirty cop and not snitching on one of your own. What good is that?" Lancett put a finger to his chin and averted his eyes upwards. "Albeit I'm sure the lions thought he tasted good."

That bit of news did not sit too well with Craig. The tension knot in the back of his neck made its presence, but it would have to subside without his help.

"In the time I have been acquainted with you, Lancett, I thought you were better than the ruthless drug Cartel you work for." Craig had to keep him talking while he devised a plan for rescuing the sisters and keeping himself alive long enough to do it.

Lancett heaved a heavy sigh. "I guess the five years with DeVore rubbed off on me a bit." The corners of his mouth turned up. "The best thing that happened to me. Otherwise, I would still be getting paid *peanuts* from the Mullicans." Distaste hit in his last sentence.

"Didn't pay you enough, I gather."

"No, they didn't. They threw thousands on those two spoiled brats. Rose on her unicorn stuff, and Susan on her expensive schooling in Louisiana. I tried to persuade Susan to marry me, so I could gain access to their money. But she turned me down."

Lancett came closer to Craig. "You two shared the same house together. Tell me, did she give up her body to you?" A smirk crossed his face.

Craig had no intentions of answering that question, merely glared at him.

"Not going to kiss and tell, huh. Or are you still heartbroken over the death of your wife? You do know I did you a favor by having her killed, don't you? You don't want strings attached in the drug business. Amusing that DeVore considered it a two for one, since she was pregnant with your baby. I got paid double." Lancett's teeth emerged as his grin grew bigger.

"You son of a..." Craig lunged at Lancett, causing him to jump backwards.

Ginger grabbed a hold of Craig's belt and pulled him towards her. Her gun jabbed into his side.

"Settle down, Summers," she gritted through her tensed lips.

"Yes, you better do what the lady says, Summers. I have heard her trigger finger is sensitive." Lancett gave out a heckle.

Craig's heart raced, but he had more questions to ask. He needed to clear his mind of the pain Lancett and DeVore put on him by taking Lillian and their unborn son's life.

"Considering you're getting paid so much for the drugs, why fixate on selling it to the kids? Why not the adults? They possess more cash to buy the heroin, and you would take in more money." Craig played on the greedy side of Lancett.

A devilish grin danced on Lancett's face. "DeVore flooded that market. He wanted me to start them at a young age, so to say. When I would take Rose to those handy-me-down places to search for her toys, I detected a majority of kids working in the back. After talking to the owners of some stores, I realized they were looking for some extra money on the side."

"Underhandedly, I assume."

"You are correct. And you played in the plan perfectly, using you for the auctions by telling you what to purchase, so the heroin would wind up at the facilities. At the time I had the impression you were an accountant for the drug Cartel. It was not until later when DeVore asked me about you I realized different. Shame on you." Lancett wagged his finger at Craig.

"Shame on me? Shame on you. When did selling drugs turn into kid-napping?" Craig wanted to know the reason behind the extra activity.

"Ever since Susan wouldn't marry me. I could not grab on to the company any other way. I thought after her parents' deaths she would relin-quish it to me. But, no, that greedy spoiled brat wouldn't do it." Lancett's expression hardened as steam came pouring out of his ears.

A shipmate came up the stairs and whispered something in Lancett's ear.

"Can she walk yet?" Lancett asked the man.

"Barely."

Craig was sure they were either talking about Susan or Rose. He had to find a way to reach them.

Lancett looked around the cabin before setting his gaze upon Craig.

"You will excuse me for a few minutes. One of my guests is having a hard time getting out of bed." Lancett scorned. "I'll return soon. Entertain yourselves while I'm gone." He gave a broad smile, and the shipmates chuckled.

Lancett disappeared down the steps. Craig tried to wrench away from Ginger, and follow Lancett, but she pulled him back and under her breath told him to play it cool.

His gut churned even more, while his imagination ran away with him. Lancett asking the shipmate if she could walk yet and telling Craig one of his *guests* had a hard time getting out of bed did not sit too well with him. He hated thinking about what Lancett was capable of doing to Susan considering all the animosity he had against her.

If Craig made it out alive, he would put a target on Lancett's back. Not if, but when, he corrected himself. No way he would go down without a fight, and Lancett would be in his line of fire. He would make sure of it.

Lancett appeared back on the steps and on the deck.

"Well, apparently Larry was telling the truth. She can hardly walk. Let alone stand. So, since the plans about the plane changed with the FBI going out to the airport, I'll have to be rid of them in another way."

Lancett focused his attention on Craig. "And you as well. That will be more of a pleasure." His smile was more of a smirk.

"James, if you would take Mr. Summers from Ginger..."

"I've got Summers," Ginger broke in. "I have been waiting a long time for this day. What do you want me to do with him?"

Surprise lit up Lancett's face, then replaced with satisfaction.

"Let me guess. A scorned woman after revenge, Ginger?"

She looked Lancett up and down once. "Something like that."

"You sound like my kind of woman. Bring him down here. I want to watch his reactions to seeing the girls killed before him. James, come with us. You are awarded the honors to do away with the sisters." Evil was written all over Lancett.

Ginger poked Craig, pushing him in Lancett's direction. He obeyed without hesitation.

A galley exposed itself to them once they made it down the flight of stairs. Lancett rounded the staircase, taking them through a narrow hallway. Bunkers appeared through the opened doors. They stopped in a cleared area.

"Well, Summers, you wanted to examine the cargo hold. Here's one of them."

Lancett and James stood in front of Craig with Ginger holding her gun steady in Craig's side.

"Go help Larry with the girls." Lancett kept his eyes on Craig while James went through a metal door to an adjoining enclosure. The door opened back up, and Craig waited in anticipation for the sisters to pop through it.

A stringy haired, fragile Rose came through first with Larry holding on to her arm. She looked like she had been drugged. He cringed at the thought of her being kept in that condition for over a year.

Next Susan stumbled out with James' arm around her waist, trying to keep her on her bare feet. His eyes zeroed in on Susan's appearance. Her auburn hair in shambles. Her vibrant blue sundress scoffed up, with the top button unfastened. Fire heated up his insides. He knew Lancett had undressed her.

"So, you include rape into your drug dealings as well?" Craig forced out past clenched teeth.

Lancett laughed. "Why the concern, my friend? It's not like you were banging her." He raised a brow. "Or were you?" Irritation hit in his last words.

Craig turned his attention back to Susan. She bobbed her head up. Through her glazed over eyes, he saw a spark of recognition dawn in them. A faint smile played with her lips.

Chapter 26

Was Susan dreaming? Revisiting her nightmare she had in her apartment? Lots of water, Rose, John, Craig, and someone with a handgun were in it. What about the ending? She remembered it was traumatic.

And who held her by the waist? It sure as heck was not Craig. He stood in front of her. Her eyes must be deceiving her. Was Ginger pointing a gun on Craig?

Wake up, Susan!

"What's going on?" Susan asked groggily.

John turned in her direction. His sinister smile brought her back to reality. He had drugged her with heroin by thrashing the narcotic down her throat with his finger. She pushed away the arm holding her up and stumbled to the floor.

"Stand her back up, James." John's voice was drilling out the orders. Susan fought off James' attempts, and straggled back up on her own, bracing herself against the wall. She was woozy, but she did not want another man touching her.

"Stubborn to the end, eh, Susan?" John gave a snicker.

"Why, why did you do this, John? Why did you kidnap Rose?" If this was it for her, she wanted some answers. At least when she died, she would know why.

John casually walked the few steps to Susan. He put his right arm above her head, leaning on the metal, and with his left hand he raised her chin up, bringing them eye level.

A commotion caught her attention, and out of the corner of her eyes she saw Ginger holding Craig back.

"Quite simple, sweetie. You refused to marry me. You see, if you would have, there would be no need for this." He smiled down into her face.

She shook her head in his hand. "I still don't understand."

He puckered his lips. After removing his hand from her face, he moved away from her, straightening himself up.

"I guess, since you're going to cease to exist anyways, it doesn't matter if I tell you." He paused for moment. "Unless you want to go in partnership with me and save you and your sister?" He cocked an eyebrow at her, giving her a lopsided grin. He peered over at Craig. "Summers will still die," he grunted.

She focused on Craig's face. His irises were an eerie black. She did not want him shot to death, or her and Rose. There had to be some way of saving all three of them.

"What's in it for you if I marry you?" She would never wed him now, but she needed to bide some time for them. She prayed Craig had a plan to bring them safely out of the predicament, and Ginger putting a gun to him was part of it.

Amusement danced on John's face. "A couple of reasons. One of them is having my way with you." The hunger in his eyes almost frightened Susan. He towered over her like a wolf about to dig into its prey.

"I observed you for ten years go from a scrawny little teenage girl to a well-formed woman." His eyes surveyed her up and down, showing his cynical grin. "You never knew I had put cameras in your room, did you?"

"I never figured you to be a pervert, Lancett," Craig spewed out.

John winced as though Craig threw a brick at his head before turning in his direction.

"There is a lot about me you don't know, Summers. I placed those minicams after the tragic accident of Rose and Susan's parents plane crash. After moving into the house with the girls, I wanted to make sure they were secure."

"Sounds more like the only one they needed guarding against was you," Craig batted back.

"Oh, on the contrary, my dear friend. Did Susan ever tell you about her prom date? How he forced himself on her, then threw her out of the car like a piece of trash when she fought off his advances?" John turned his head in Susan's direction, raising a brow at her.

Susan had not told anyone about that night, other than John. Her cheeks became warm. The humiliation she went through flooded back. She glanced at Craig, and a muscle in his jaw twitched.

John returned his attention back to Craig. "I took care of the weasel. Somehow he winded up in a gang fight." The amusement in John's voice rang clear.

"You, you killed him?" The knowledge of John killing another person became a scary reality. She found herself sliding down the wall.

In an instant John walked her back up on her feet. She glared into his eyes. Darkness replaced his brilliant blue color irises.

"How many other people did you kill?" It was an answer she did not want to hear but asked anyway.

"For you, sweetie, one other. Remember the sleaze ball in college you dated? He dumped you and spread rumors around about how easy it was to sack you in the bed." John's face twisted with a wry smile.

Susan groaned. "Is that why he never showed back up at school?"

She started sliding back down. John took hold of her hands, holding them above her head, and pulling her back up.

"I guess in a way you could say I loved you. I was outraged over those two clowns for touching my sweetie."

A devilish grin latched on to his face as he lowered himself to devour her lips. When she did not yield her mouth for him, he bit her lower lip. He plunged his tongue deep inside as she caved in to cry out in pain. Pinned between John's body and the wall made it impossible for her to move away from him.

He withdrew his mouth from hers. "Too bad I couldn't influence you to love me," he said raising his head.

She went to knee him in the crotch. Before she made an impact, he closed his legs around her oncoming thigh.

"Uh, uh, uh. Don't forget, I was in your karate classes with you. I am familiar with your moves." A broad smile came on his face.

She glared at him, lowering her leg as he released the tension on it.

"Tell me why you kidnapped me." Rose wrenched out of the man's hold and charged at John. John immediately let go of Susan and backed up.

"Grab her, Larry!" John said through clenched teeth. Larry jerked Rose back by her elbows.

Susan came off the wall, and James pushed her back, knocking the wind out of her.

"Seems the only one around here who can control their charge is Ginger." John walked over to Ginger. "You're the type of woman I need on my team."

Ginger gave John a crooked smile. "I hold my own."

"Other than thinking you would have a chance of getting in my pants, what was the other reason for taking Rose?"

John turned back around. "Well, if you really want the scoop, it's to take over the company."

"You carry the president seat. Isn't that enough?"

"No!" John's roar startled her, causing her to jump out of her skin.

He regained his composure. "You see, sweetie, the firm is worth a lot of money. Jeremy, a businessman, wanted to buy it from your parents. For some reason they refused to sell to him. After Mr. and Mrs. Mullican died, I was going to liquidate it so you and Rose could have a hefty inheritance." He put on a fake smile.

"But you only *allowed* me to manage the business. If you married me, I would have offered it to Jeremy. Since you would not do that, I had to go this route to wrangle the plant from you." Sternness hit with his last sentence.

Susan remembered Craig saying something about a Jeremy at his house in Summersville when he asked her if anyone tried to obtain the corporation. It now occurred to her what John planned to do.

"You were going to give my parents company to that drug lord?" Disgust hit her gut.

John waved his hand in the air. "I have a different viewpoint. It would have been a business deal. Whatever he decided to do with the orchards would be up to him."

"And how was keeping Rose from me going to help you gain the company?" She glared at John.

"Well, since you still refused to marry me, I had to entice you down here with Rose."

Craig broke in. "Is that why you planted the blue folder in my office?"

The corners of John's mouth quirked up. He retained eye contact with Susan as he answered Craig. "Yes, yes, it is. I figured this was an adequate way to abolish you too." He faced Craig.

"I had different plans of disposing of you. I had not contemplated on the feds coming, so they spoiled my original idea of getting rid of the two *snotty brats.*"

"You mean by taking them up in the airplane, and killing them in Dallas?" Craig's confusion was evident.

An evil laugh escaped John. "No. The plane was going to crash for a second time."

"What!?" Had Susan heard John right.

He spun around so quick it almost made her dizzy.

"That is the same plane which crashed with your parents on board, sweetie. I had the scraps, along with some new parts, like the engine, put together like a jigsaw puzzle." Evil inhabited his face.

"That's ludicrous! Don't you have any respect?"

"Oh, about as much as when I sabotaged it the first time."

The words came at her like a bulldozer. "What do you mean you sabotaged it?"

"The day they left for your birthday they were supposed to go to a meeting with some people interested in merging with your parents' company. That would have been disastrous if Frank and Francis signed those papers. So, I took care of their trip."

John held a smirk on his face. Susan lunged at him. He caught hold of her wrists and slung her against the wall with his body causing her breath to be forced out. Sounds of stirring behind John and a very audible ugh coming from Craig reached her ears.

John crossed her fingers with his, crushing them, causing excruciating pain.

"I think I'll just take you now."

In one swift moment John grasped and yanked her summer dress, causing the buttons to spring off the front, and held her hands prisoner again. Susan screamed before he crushed their lips together and pushed himself into her. The pain searing through her body from his sudden impact on her caused her heart throbbing to increase through her head.

She became weak from lack of oxygen to her brain. Black spots danced in her vision. A gunshot rang out as she went limp, and she felt something warm run down her skin. The whole room went black as she slid down on to the floor.

Chapter 27

A stinging sensation ran up Susan's nostrils, and she tried to move her face away from the stench. She blinked open her eyes, oblivious to what had happened. Until she looked down and noticed blood on her. She started hyperventilating as pictures flashed through her mind of the scene before she blacked out.

"Hey, sugar, it's all right." A set of strong arms gently rocked her with a soothing voice. Craig held her, calming her down.

"Did you kill him?" She peered up into his eyes.

Distaste fell on his lips. "No," he said. "I only wounded his right shoulder."

She was relieved. At once her thoughts went to Rose. Susan scrambled out of his embrace. "Where's Rose?" She surveyed every inch of the room for her.

"She's being treated at the hospital, which is where you need to go." He motioned to the paramedics standing by.

"What about you?" She did not want to leave Craig's side.

"I'll be there soon." He gave her a reassuring smile.

The ambulance attendant helped Susan walk to the stairs and off the boat to a waiting gurney on the deck. She laid down while they strapped her in, thinking back to the past week when she started at The Five and Dime Store. So much had happened, and she would have some sorting out to do now that Rose was found.

Most of all her feelings about Craig. How could she envision life beyond his line of duty? Never knowing if he kills somebody, or worse, gets impaired himself. Was her love for him strong enough to accept his profession?

* * *

Craig stayed behind with Ginger and a couple of other officers. They gave their statements to the commanding officer, and she handed over her cam.

"You'll find everything we need, as well as what the FBI and DEA needs for their investigation," Ginger confirmed.

"A job well done. I'm glad that bunch of drug Cartel are off our streets." The lieutenant displayed a grim smile on his face. "The sad thing is it won't be long before another group comes to take their place."

"We'll be prepared for them, sir," she said with an affirmation. She turned to Craig and asked him if he was ready to exit off the barge.

"I'll meet you at the station," he replied. Ginger nodded then she and the others made their way down the hallway.

Craig stood in the cargo hold for a few minutes taking in everything Lancett had proclaimed. Lancett tearing Susan's dress, and about to rape her caused him to snap. He wanted to kill the sleaze ball, but fear of the bullet hitting Susan deterred that decision.

Ginger left the gun in his back as planned. It was tough not using the pistol at an earlier time, but it was mandatory to draw out the goods on Lancett. And Lancett gave them everything they needed.

He had to give praise to Sergeant Garcia for some quick thinking up on deck when Lancett told James to take him down the stairs. It would have put a kink in the plans. Thankfully, the officers already arrested the shipmates, and were close by waiting to take down Lancett, Larry, and James when he shot Lancett.

"There you are Craig."

He turned around to identify who the voice belonged to. Randall and Tony made their way inside the cargo hold.

"We learned missy got roughed up. How's she doing?" Concern filled Randall's face. Tony was equally worried. They only spent a couple of days with Susan, but it was not hard to care about a sweet soul like hers.

"The paramedics took her to the hospital an hour or two ago. I am about to head there myself. You two are more than welcomed to join me. I'm sure she'll love to see you guys."

Their faces lit up. "What are we waiting for," came Tony's reply.

They evacuated the boat in haste and climbed into Randall's Sedan.

"So, did it shake Lancett up when he was told the FBI was on their way out to the airport?" Randall addressed Craig.

"To say the least. That bit of news kept him on board the ship."

Randall nodded. "It did its job."

"The footage Sergeant Ginger Garcia took with her police cam will do wonders for the case. Mr. Lancett will be incarcerated for a few lifetimes with all he did." Tony wore a smile from ear to ear.

"Always feels good to put the likes of him away for a long time," Randall added.

The satisfaction of catching Lancett prevailed as a win. His main fish to catch was Jeremy DeVore. With the evidence they acquired, it would not take long to reel him in.

The hospital loomed in front of them. Craig was eager to lay eyes on Susan, but also hesitant. They would be going their separate ways with Rose being found. He was not sure if he wanted to say goodbye to her yet.

Female laughter filled the hallway as the three men neared the sisters' hospital room. Craig stuck his head in the doorway and relieved to discover them in good spirits.

Rose caught sight of him. Recognition came upon her face. "Hey, I remember you. You were the accountant at the store I worked at."

Susan turned in his direction. She was as giddy as a schoolgirl on her fist date.

"Yes, and if not for him, as well as two men I hope are behind him," she raised her eyes to peek around him, "are the ones who helped me find you."

Randall and Tony made their debut into the room.

"Yes," Susan clapped. "The tall slender guy is Tony."

Tony bowed his head in Rose's direction.

"And our wise owl is Randall," she announced. Rose gave her a quizzical expression. "I'll explain later."

"It's good to meet you. We are about to leave town, but wanted to visit you first, missy." Randall aimed the last sentence to Susan.

Susan averted her attention to Craig. "Are you leaving as well?" Sorrow soaked in her voice.

Craig longed to hold her and tell her he would be by her side forever.

But he could not make a promise like that to her. He knew her reaction about guns, and he was not certain if he could walk away from four generations of law enforcement.

"I'm afraid so. I have to return to the base and close up this case."

"Well, can I at least persuade a hug from all three of you?" Her words quivered some, but she remained strong.

"You bet, missy." Randall's face brightened as he made a mad dash to her.

"Do I get one too?" Rose stuck out her arms. Tony embraced her first. Afterwards, he and Randall traded off sisters.

Craig encompassed Rose first. He wanted his lasting impression of holding someone to be Susan.

She still retained a faint fragrance of Red. He took in one big whiff of her before releasing his embrace around her.

God, he was going to miss her!

* * *

"Here you go, Charlie." Susan took in the broad smile on her little patient as he held the blow fish mask up to his face with delight.

"Ms. Susan, when can we wear these masks?" Marcella inquired as she sported her mermaid face around.

Susan glanced over at her bleached-blonde co-worker. "I don't know. We'll have to ask Ms. Betty. What do you say?"

Before Betty answered, a knock on the opened door of the play area startled them. They both turned their attention to the person knocking.

Susan's heart sank. A month had passed since she last beheld the golden-eyes, Stetson wearing, masculine man. And that did not include the breathtaking dreams of him.

She wanted to jump right into his arms but refrained herself. Especially in front of the children.

"Well, hello tall, dark, and handsome." Betty crossed the room to Craig. "I bet I can identify who you are." She winked at Susan. "He's better looking in person than the way you described him. I'm Betty Trublood by the way. Nice to finally meet you."

Susan boosted herself from the small chair at the table and steadied her wobbling legs on her way over to a slightly embarrassed Craig.

"I hope I'm not interrupting anything?"

Somehow, she found her voice. "No, no. Not at all. We were fixing masks for a party we're putting on."

Little Joey came up between them, holding his shark mask in one hand while tugging on Craig's hand with the one which donned an arm cast. Craig crouched down to Joey's level.

"What do you have there?" He asked as Joey put on his disguise.

"I'm a shark. Chomp, chomp."

Craig chuckled. Standing up, he scanned around the room. "Let me see. Shark, blow fish, and a mermaid. Where's the squid?"

"Here I am!" Robert came hobbling in from the hallway on his crutches, displaying his squid face with pride.

Betty squinted her eyes. "How did you know about the squid?"

Craig's face twisted. "You mean you haven't told her about the masquerade masks you did not make for the celebration?"

Susan's face began getting warm. She was surprised he remembered about those. "No."

"Not yet" Betty tossed in. "Look, why don't you two go out to the patio and do some catching up. I'll cover for you, girl."

Susan led him out the double glass doors and motioned for him to take a seat on the bench.

Craig wet his lips before speaking. "I went by your place to drop off the unicorn carousel you left back in Port Emerald. You were not there, so I gave it to Rose. I hope you don't mind?"

Susan had forgotten about the gift she bought at the auction. "Not at all. I'm not going to ask how you knew where I live at." Her laughter brought out a sparkling smile from Craig. She remembered kissing those lips. Part of her, most of her, wanted to partake of them again.

"Rose showed me her unicorn collection. The funny thing is the lamp she has used to be mine. I had put my initials on its bottom years ago." He gazed into her eyes.

"That is odd."

"I also came by to tell you about Lancett."

Susan's heart quickened. The dreadful time with him resurfaced. "He's not out on bond, is he?"

Craig's facial expression changed. "No, they're not about to grant him one. You and Rose, however, will need to testify at the hearing." A somber gaze overtook his appearance.

"I understand." With a heavy sigh she asked when the trial would be.

"A couple of more months. More evidence is still needed on him. We will require some information from your parents' business."

"Yes, of course. Did Rose tell you we are selling it?"

"Yes. To a cotton grower, I believe is what she said."

Susan nodded. "We didn't want to sell it as is. Did not want to take the chance of getting into the wrong hands. Again."

Relief was written on Craig's face. He looked toward the building they exited. "I am delighted you got your old job back." The corners of his mouth turned up. He waved at the children looking on at them.

His countenance became serious as he turned his head, eyeing Susan directly in the face. He pulled out a piece of paper from his shirt pocket which had a familiarity about it.

"Did you mean what you wrote in this note?"

Her eyes enlarged. "Oh my gosh! You kept that from last year?" She grimaced. "Actually, they've changed."

Sadness clouded his features.

"I didn't know you as well at that time. As I became better acquainted with you, and since you are not on the wrong side of the law, I could absolutely fall for you."

His gorgeous smile found its way back in place. "I'm pleased to hear that because I have fallen for you. I will be submitting a two weeks' notice and land a regular job. One where guns and danger are not involved."

"I can't ask that of you. I know what it means to you to lock up criminals."

Craig reached over, and casually brushed a stray strand of hair away from her eyes. "I love you, Susan, and I want to do this. I want you to be my wife."

Her insides fluttered. "There is only one way I will marry you." His eyes sparked with inquiry. "Continue being a DEA officer. I love you for who you are, not what you are."

He drew her in to him, and she accepted the kiss with loving eagerness.

A knocking on a window caused her to cut short from the embrace. Betty stood at the glass door, pointing down to the children. Embarrassment ran into her face. "Can I meet with you after work?" she requested.

"For the rest of our lives, I hope."

"You can believe that. I'd be crazy to let you go."